"I don't want an affair with you!"

It was bad enough working for Cosmo's aunt and living in his house without this! He knew full well the power he had to arouse her.

"You know, Dawn, you are one woman I don't understand very well." Cosmo sighed, still holding her, his eyes searching hers.

She didn't know how to answer without revealing too much.

"Dear God, you are beautiful, Dawn." His arms tightened around her and then there was his voice again, soft and gentle, his lips brushing lightly against her ear. "And if I told you that I love you, would it make any difference?"

In that instant she almost hated him. Dawn knew Cosmo's feelings about love. And she would never have believed he would resort to lies, to get her into his bed.

CLAUDIA JAMESON lives in Berkshire, England, with her husband and family. She is an extremely popular author in both the Harlequin Presents and Harlequin Romance series. And no wonder! Her lively dialogue and ingenious plots—with the occasional dash of suspense—make her a favorite with romance readers everywhere.

Books by Claudia Jameson

These books may be available at your local bookseller.

Don't miss any of our special offers. Write to us at the following address for information on our newest releases.

Harlequin Reader Service
901 Fuhrmann Blvd., P.O. Box 1397, Buffalo, NY 14240
Canadian address: P.O. Box 2800, Postal Station A,
5170 Yonge St., Willowdale, Ont. M2N 6J3

CLAUDIA JAMESON

the man in room 12

Harlequin Books

TORONTO • NEW YORK • LONDON
AMSTERDAM • PARIS • SYDNEY • HAMBURG
STOCKHOLM • ATHENS • TOKYO • MILAN

Harlequin Presents first edition June 1986
ISBN 0-373-10891-5

Original hardcover edition published in 1985
by Mills & Boon Limited

CHAPTER ONE

DUSK was rapidly closing in, the surrounding hills were hazy shapes of grey in the whiteness of the blizzard, and the snow that had been falling continuously all afternoon was now being whipped into a froth by a vicious wind which howled eerily around the old building.

Dawn Davies got to her feet and closed the curtains in the tiny reception area of the Glendale Inn. It had been a long time since Snowdonia National Park had been blanketed this thickly in snow. But the weather was foul not only in Wales—the whole of Britain had been buffeted and belted by gale force winds, treacherous rainstorms or snowfalls. Scotland was suffering most; every night for the past ten days there had been pictures and reports on television of the havoc being wreaked in Scotland, and for the past couple of days Wales had been getting her share. Roofs had been blown off barns, trees had come crashing down and animals were suffering, getting lost or dying of starvation. Drivers had been abandoning their cars, getting trapped in snowdrifts or queueing for hours in traffic jams on roads which were passable but congested because of accidents. Ah, but how different this countryside was in the summer! How the tourists came in droves to enjoy the dramatic sight of Mount Snowdon and the myriad other attractions Wales had to offer.

'Tea's up!' Shirley Davies poked her head around the door of the family living room which led off from reception. 'Dawn? Come on, it's time you had a break. You're supposed to be on holiday, you know. You didn't come here to work!'

'I'm happy to help out, Mum.' Dawn slipped the plastic cover over the old manual typewriter, pulled a dying leaf off the poinsettia on the reception counter and followed her mother into the living room. She was privately worrying about the Hobday family; they had gone off in their car several hours ago and they should have been back by now. They always came back in time for tea. Still, she wouldn't say anything to her mother just yet. She was probably worrying needlessly. Mr Hobday must know the surrounding roads almost as well as Dawn herself did. For the past nine years he, his wife and two teenage sons had stayed at the inn for the first week of the New Year and for the first two weeks of August. His sons had been rowdy little boys when they'd first come to stay.

Apart from the Hobdays and Miss Williams, who lived at the inn, there were only two other guests at the moment. It was by no means a full house, the inn having twelve guest bedrooms, but it wasn't bad for the time of year, especially in view of the weather. How many people wanted to take a January holiday in a small country inn in the middle of nowhere in weather like this? Of course Snowdonia was beautiful, extremely so, but one couldn't see anything of it at the moment!

'I've been surprised by the number of enquiries we've had for next season. Your little advert in the *Radio Times* has worked wonders, Mum. Or do you suppose that this horrible weather is making everyone think ahead to their summer holiday? I mean, to the extent that they're actually getting down to booking there and then?'

'All I know is that we're going to have a very

successful season. You must have answered dozens of enquiries since you've been here.'

'And I bet there'd have been more in today's post.' Dawn took the cup of tea her mother handed to her and settled in the chintz armchair by the fire. Thinking ahead to the summer was all well and good but it seemed a very long way off in the midst of this freezing blizzard. Thank goodness they were very well stocked with wood and coal; if the snow continued at the rate it was falling now, the Glendale Inn was in danger of being cut off from civilisation. The post hadn't been delivered today, and that was a very bad sign. Only twice in Dawn's memory had Glendale and all its guests been snowed in, trapped, reliant entirely upon the stocks of food, drinks and fuel which were on the premises.

'I'll just take Megan a cup of tea. If she's not feeling any better, you and I will have to cope in the kitchen this evening.'

Dawn shrugged, smiling. 'No problem.' Aunty Megan was her mother's sister-in-law. Like Shirley, she was widowed, and she had lived and worked at the inn since her husband died seven years ago. One year later, Dawn's father had died of a heart attack. He had been the most unlikely candidate for a heart attack and his death had shattered not only his wife and daughter but all who had known and loved him. And to have known Glen Davies was to have loved him. He had been the nicest person Dawn had ever known. And she'd thought so not because he was her father but because it was simply the truth.

Shirley was shaking her head when she came back into the living room. 'Megan's running a high temperature. I'm afraid we've got another victim on our hands.'

'Flu. It was rife at the moment. The bartender had been in bed with it for the past three days, not that there was any passing trade as far as the bar was concerned! The chambermaid who lived in also had 'flu, and now Aunty Megan was ill. And it was Aunt Megan who did all the cooking.

'I suppose she won't let you send for the doctor?'

Shirley lowered herself tiredly into a chair, looking worried. 'Of course not. But at least she's promised to stay put, so that's something.'

'It means she's feeling rotten.' Dawn smiled grimly. Aunty Megan was a tough, hardworking lady and if she'd promised to stay in bed, it meant she was feeling *ill*. 'Don't look so worried, Mum, she'll be all right in a few days.'

'Oh, it isn't that.' Shirley waved a hand in acceptance of the statement. 'It's you. You're supposed to be having a rest, getting yourself together, and you've done nothing but work since you've been here. I didn't intend you to clean rooms and wait on tables and serve drinks and——'

'I've told you, I'm happy to help.'

'You're a good girl, Dawn. Now why don't you take a quick nap while you've got the chance?' And with that, Shirley took her own advice and closed her eyes.

Dawn smiled as she watched her mother drift quickly into a light sleep, then turned her attention to the dancing flames of the fire, not in the least tired herself. In fact she was vaguely amused by the running around she'd had to do during the past few days. Having been brought up in the business, there was no aspect of the running of the inn that she couldn't cope with. It was just that she'd had to change hats so often since she'd been here—playing receptionist one minute, barmaid the next—and tonight she'd be commis chef to her mother!

But she hadn't come home for a rest, actually, she had come home to think. She had lived at the inn all her life, that was until she left for college at the age of seventeen—just six months after her father had died. She had gone to Manchester then, and although the city was only an hour's drive from North Wales it had seemed like a different world to Dawn, who had been used to wide open spaces, beautiful scenery, fresh air and a quiet life. The three-year course she'd taken in art and design had developed the artistic talent she had been born with and equipped her very well indeed for any number of jobs as a commercial artist.

If only she could find the *right* job.

If only she could find the right job, in the right place.

After leaving college, she had worked for a year in the art department of an advertising agency in Manchester. Maybe she should have stayed there instead of moving on to London, thinking she would find the capital exciting, interesting, challenging.

Well, to be fair, it *had* been all those things—for a few weeks. But as soon as she'd started work as an illustrator on a magazine, commuting halfway across the city to Fleet Street every day, London had lost its charm. True, she had coped with the pressure she'd worked under on the magazine, but she hadn't enjoyed it. She did not thrive on pressure, she did not produce her best work in those circumstances, either.

Visiting London was one thing; working there was quite another. She had found it too noisy, too crowded, and the pace of life in the capital was . . . impossible as far as Dawn was concerned. Maybe it was just too much of a contrast to her beloved Wales? No, it wasn't that, because she didn't want to stay here for long, either.

Sighing inwardly, she let her eyes close, though her

mind was busily analysing and leaping ahead. In a couple of months she would be twenty-three years old . . . where would she be then? What would she be doing? At her age, she felt, she ought to know exactly what it was that she wanted from life. But she didn't, not quite. Nor was she depressed about it. Depression was almost an unknown emotion to Dawn, ever the optimist.

So what if she had given up two perfectly good jobs? Neither of them, or neither of the cities she had worked in, she wasn't quite sure which, had been right for her. Currently she was scanning the papers every day, hoping to find something in Swansea or Cardiff. It would be ideal to have easy access to beautiful countryside while working in a job which made use of her artistic talents. That would give her the best of both worlds.

The slamming of the front door broke her train of thought. Shirley's eyes came open as Dawn got quickly to her feet. 'What is it, darling?'

'The Hobdays, I hope. I've been worrying about them.' Dawn glanced at her watch as she headed for the door to reception. 'It's pitch black outside now and the snow's never stopped since . . .' Her voice trailed off as she shut the door behind her.

Shirley closed her eyes again and stretched her legs towards the fire. Having a daughter like Dawn was a great comfort to her and it was good to have her home for a while. She didn't see the girl as often as she'd have liked, but Dawn had her own life to lead and not for one moment would she try to persuade her to stay in Wales now, any more than she would have *allowed* her to stay at home after her father died. On the contrary, when Glen died and Dawn had spoken in terms of abandoning the career she wanted, to stay at home with her mother, Shirley had had to be very firm indeed. She had despatched her daughter to college in Manchester with apparent enthusiasm and with the insistence that she, Shirley, would cope perfectly well. And she had, though much of the credit for that was due to Megan.

For the hundredth time Shirley acknowledged how much of Glen's nature Dawn had inherited. She was unselfish, giving, generous to a fault. Just like Glen had been. She was hardworking, conscientious and she took everything in her stride in her own bubbly, smiling way. Unlike her father, however, Dawn did have quite a temper when pushed too far—but that temper had a very high boiling point and Shirley had only witnessed it a couple of times in the girl's twenty-three years.

Almost twenty-four years, she reflected.

Again for the hundredth time, she ached with regret that Glen had not lived to see his daughter at this stage in her life. Although she was always a pretty girl, in her early teens Dawn had been considerably overweight and her appearance had always been one of near-scruffiness despite the money she spent on clothes. Then, during her years at art school, her appearance had been—well, zany to say the least! But she had outgrown that phase, too, and now, not so many years later, she was as smart as a new pin, her figure was perfect and she was prettier than she'd ever been.

Shirley smiled to herself, but without smugness. Dawn's good looks had been inherited from her—the blonde hair, the blue eyes—though that was about all of Shirley's contribution. It was living in London, probably, that had given Dawn the polish, the touch of sophistication she had now. Whether she had enjoyed it or not, the nine months she'd spent working there had added to her, had contributed to her maturation from girl to woman.

Nevertheless, Shirley was vaguely worried about her

daughter because in spite of her apparent sophistication, she was in many ways young for her years. She was also a little vulnerable, a little too sensitive—and she was very unsettled just now.

She had given up her job and her flat in the capital and had brought all her belongings home. But she would take off again soon; Shirley was aware of that and she approved of it, too. She just hoped that the next job her daughter took would be the right one, one that would satisfy whatever it was that burned, unsatisfied, within her. On the other hand, maybe what she needed to make her happy was not a job at all . . . Had there been a man in Dawn's life for any length of time, she'd have suggested the idea of settling down to marriage. But there hadn't been a man in Dawn's life. There had been dozens—but no one man in particular.

The entire Hobday family were standing on the big, square doormat behind the solid wooden door of the inn. Dawn grinned broadly then gurgled with laughter as they stomped their feet and banged their hands together and shivered and moaned. 'Am I glad to see you! I was getting quite worried about you! What happened?'

Mrs Hobday merely shook her head, as if in disgust, the two teenage boys started saying something about what fun it had been, while their father came forward to take the keys Dawn was offering.

'The snow happened.' For once his ready smile wasn't forthcoming. 'I didn't think we'd get back. It's bloody awful out there, Dawn, and I won't be surprised if we can't get away tomorrow.'

Dawn suppressed a smile. Mr Hobday was very down to earth (something which irritated old Miss Williams no end, most especially when he swore) and he would no doubt give the old lady a graphic account of his experiences in the snow when they met up in the television room later on. 'You must look on the bright side. Maybe there'll be a change in the weather. It has to happen somctime!'

She handed over the keys to their rooms, laughed at the grunt she got in reply and suggested they all took a hot bath and had a pot of tea. All the rooms had tea-making facilities in them—though Miss Williams always took her afternoon tea in the lounge.

With that in mind, Dawn looked at her watch again and headed for the kitchens. Miss Williams was a lonely old dear who had no relatives, who loved company and looked forward to having a chat with Dawn whenever possible. She was in fact Dawn's old teacher from primary school and the two were very fond of each other. Miss Williams had retired only three years earlier and had lived at the Glendale Inn from that day on.

From six o'clock onwards neither Dawn nor her mother had time to think about anything. The young couple in room five complained that their bedroom radiator was stone cold, Mr Hobday came in search of a new light bulb for the boys' room and mentioned in passing that the younger one had started sneezing, there was a sootfall in the television room, and dinner had to be prepared, cooked and served to all the guests. To cap it all, Dawn and her mother found themselves coping entirely alone. Glenys, a local part-timer who came in at mealtimes, telephoned from her home in the village to say that her son was down with measles and she wouldn't be coming in.

Since the other waitress-cum-chambermaid was in bed with the 'flu, as was the barman-cum-handyman, who also lived in, it was just as well there were so few guests and no passing trade! But they coped; neither Shirley nor Dawn were the type to panic when thrown

in at the deep end, and Dawn saw firstly to her aunt
and the two staff who were ill, before buckling down in
the kitchens.

The entire evening was one long, hectic run-around
and by ten o'clock Dawn was tired out—though she
wouldn't admit it to her mother, who was even more
tired.

All the guests had been understanding of the
proprietress' predicament and staff-shortage, and by ten
o'clock the young couple from room five were in the
bar which was being manned—intermittently—by
Shirley, the Hobdays were still in the dining room
lingering over their coffee, and at that point Dawn saw
her opportunity to go and clear the sootfall in the TV
room. The room couldn't be used until the mess had
been cleaned up, so Miss Williams had settled in the
residents' lounge with her mug of cocoa and was
playing patience until her bedtime.

'Mum, there's only the coffee cups to see to. I've
cleared the kitchens and set the tables for breakfast—all
but the Hobdays'—so I'll just clean up that soot and
then I'll call it a day.'

'No, Dawn, leave it.' Shirley was fishing change out
of the till behind the bar. 'I'll do it early in the
morning.'

'Certainly not.' Dawn was firm. '*I'll* do it. *Now.*' She
smiled and shook her head at her mother's searching
look. 'Honestly, I'm fine, I'm not in the least tired. Why
don't you get yourself a drink, close up here and go to
bed—you've earned it!'

Her mother didn't argue.

The Glendale Inn was a homely, comfortable,
rambling old house full of character with its chintzy
furniture, its warm, subdued lighting, its roaring fires
and copper and brass ornaments—but there was a lot

of work involved in maintaining its charming appearance. Every morning, someone had to make the fires. Someone had to hoover the old, richly-coloured carpets. Someone had to polish the copper and brass, and it was with all this in mind that Dawn promised herself an early night—as soon as she'd cleared the soot. She slipped into her bedroom and quickly changed into a pair of denims and an old sweater before tackling it.

It took far longer than she expected. Powdery black dust was everywhere, in every nook and cranny of the room, and she was obliged to hoover everything, curtains and furniture included. She then rolled up her sleeves and plunged her hands into a bucket of hot, soapy water and started washing the fireplace. Down the chimney came the incessant noise of the wind and small particles of the remaining soot which floated towards the warmth of her perspiring face. She was sweating as though it were midsummer by the time she'd finished.

By then it was almost midnight. So much for her early night! Still, she thought as she headed towards the kitchens, better to do it now than at six in the morning! She ran a hand tiredly across her forehead, shoving away the blonde hair which was sticking to her skin. She kept her hair short, cut into a bubbly style which framed her face beautifully—when it was clean!

And that was about all there remained to do, she acknowledged with satisfaction as she headed across the hallway to the family's quarters. Just lock up, take a bath and then fall into—

Even as she'd been thinking about locking up, she'd wondered whether her mother had already done it. Evidently she hadn't, because the front door suddenly opened so swiftly, so hard that it slammed back on its hinges and a broad, stocky figure of a man stepped inside, bringing with him a blast of wind and a scattering of snow which tumbled on to the doormat.

Dawn simply stood there and gaped at him.

He looked frozen stiff, he flung an overnight bag to the floor and stood, stomping his feet and banging his gloved hands together just as the Hobdays had done earlier in the day. For long seconds he seemed unable to speak and he was staring at Dawn in much the same way she was staring at him—as though another human being were the last thing either of them had expected to see at this time of night.

A motorist who'd run into trouble. As her brain jerked into action and she smiled in welcome, realising he might have been walking for miles, the man barked at her so harshly that she jumped.

'Don't just stand there, girl! Can't you see I'm nearly frozen to death? This is a hotel, isn't it?'

'I—yes. Well, it's an inn, the Glendale Inn. Did you want a room for the night? Are you in trouble?' She moved, quickly, to get behind the reception desk, changing her hat to that of receptionist whilst looking very much like a chimney sweep. If she'd known quite how awful she looked, she'd have been very embarrassed indeed.

But Dawn was too intrigued by his looks to think about her own. His lean face was deeply suntanned and it seemed so incongruous in this climate that she stared at him again without realising she was doing so. He had stepped up to the reception desk, was still clenching and unclenching his hands, scowling at her as she watched in fascination the snow which was perched on his thick black hair and on his eyebrows, snow which was just beginning to melt now in the warmth of the building. Then her gaze moved down fractionally and she found herself caught in the chill stare of the darkest eyes she'd ever seen.

'I am not,' he said bitingly, 'a convict on the run. Nor am I a madman who's escaped from the local loony bin. I am merely a traveller whose car has got stuck in a snowdrift, so would you kindly stop staring at me like that?'

'I'm so sorry . . .'

'Never mind that. Have you or have you not got a room?'

She smiled then. His manner did not perturb her because it was very understandable. Heaven knew how far he had walked—the inn was miles from the nearest village and main road. She could only sympathise with him. She bent her head towards the visitors' book and gave it a little push in his direction, handing him a pen as she did so. 'Yes, sir.' She smiled again, this time looking directly at him. 'There is room at the inn.'

He was not amused. He looked appalled. 'For God's sake spare me the jokes, girl!' And with that he whipped off a glove and snatched the pen from her fingers, his face taut with cold, with irritation, frustration. He signed the visitors' book swiftly, muttering to himself as he did so, 'I'm in no mood to appreciate the wit of a scruffy, stupid little parlourmaid . . .'

CHAPTER TWO

DAWN stiffened. He'd made her aware of how ridiculous she must look, covered in soot, and in fairness she had to admit what a strange sight she must be to him. But that was no reason for him to refer to her as stupid—even if she could forgive his thinking she was a parlourmaid. Still, she ignored his insult, making allowances because he must be feeling wretched. The man probably hadn't eaten for hours, had possibly even given up hope of finding shelter for the night . . .

She glanced down at the visitors' book to read his signature, determined not to react to his rudeness. 'Very well, Mr . . . Temple?' Yes, it read Temple, Cosmo, and for his address he'd put simply: Mayfair, London. She was duly impressed and she looked him over a little more carefully without making it obvious.

'I want a room with private bath,' he said then, glancing around with apparent distaste. 'I take it you do have such a thing in this twee little place? *Baths*, I mean?' There was no mistaking the pointed way he looked at her dirty face.

Dawn nodded. He was unimpressed with her *and* with the inn and that irritated her. He should be grateful that he wasn't outside dying of exposure, never mind looking with contempt at the place which was her home! Of course he didn't know that, and he was entitled to his opinion, she reminded herself.

The inn had always been run with the attitude that the customer is always right. That's what Dawn had been taught as a youngster; that's what her parents had told her over and over, though they didn't necessarily believe it. This man was not the first awkward person she'd had to deal with, nor would he be the last, so she stuck to her parents' policy and treated him with the utmost courtesy. 'Yes, sir, we have a room with a private bathroom.'

On the rack behind her was a row of keys and she reached for one. Then she paused and took instead the key to room twelve, which was the best room in the house. Beneath the cuff of the sheepskin coat the man was wearing she had seen a slim, gold Omega watch. His sweater was cashmere and his shoes were expensive, though ruined now, thanks to the snow. Apart from those tell-tale signs of money, or at least of a fine taste for things, his voice told her something about him. It was a cultured voice, every syllable he spoke coming clearly but without any affectation. It was the voice of a well-educated, confident man who was obviously used to the best in life. Well, room twelve was the best she could offer him. He could take it or leave it.

He took it.

The communal rooms and the family quarters were downstairs, all the guest rooms were upstairs, and the man followed Dawn silently, saying nothing at all until she opened the door to room twelve and switched on the main light.

'Is this the best you can do?' He spoke before he'd had time to look around, before he'd even glanced in the bathroom!

Dawn bristled but her smile didn't falter. 'The best room in the house, sir. I'm sure you'll be very comfortable——'

'Don't be.'

She glanced away from him, trying to recall whether she had ever before met someone so arrogant, so

careless of other peoples' feelings, so downright rude!
She hadn't. Well, there was a first time for everything
and she would not, she absolutely would not, answer
him back. Oh, she wasn't reminding herself now that he
was a customer, because she knew full well that he
wouldn't have set foot inside the Glendale Inn—or
anywhere as nasty—if he'd had any choice in the
matter, so it wasn't as if she could think in terms of
future business from him. It was simply that she would
not lower herself to his level. Nor would she be servile;
she would be as polite and helpful as possible, thereby
fulfilling her role and thus maintaining her dignity.

As the new guest took off his coat and flung it on a
chair Dawn turned back the coverlet on the bed whilst
pointing out the tea-making facilities. 'I'm sure you
must be longing for a cup of tea, Mr Temple. Did you
have far to walk? Is your car——'

She stopped as she turned to look at him, realising
only then that there was a great deal of anger as well as
irritation, frustration, in those grey-black eyes of his.
Loudly but with exaggerated patience, he said, 'I do *not*
want a cup of tea. I want a very large whisky, I want a
hot bath and I want some food sent up to me as quickly
as you can arrange it.' At which point he turned his
back on her and put his hands on the radiator beneath
the window.

Dawn drew a deep breath and counted to five. She
was no longer immune and she was no longer making
allowances for him. What a nerve! He really did think
her stupid! He'd spoken to her as though she were three
years old and hard of hearing to boot. Where the devil
did he think he was, the Ritz? It was on the tip of her
tongue to say this but she controlled herself. She was
not, however, about to hold a conversation with the
man while his back was turned to her!

She waited five seconds longer before addressing him because she didn't trust herself not to snap at him now. She was just as tired as he was, just as desperate for a hot bath. Besides, the inn didn't provide room service unless someone was ill; the bar was closed for the night—to non-residents and residents alike—and what did he think she could conjure up in the kitchen at twelve-thirty in the morning?

Stifling all these angry thoughts, she let her eyes flick over him. He wasn't stocky, as she'd first thought, his sheepskin coat had been responsible for that impression. He was in fact quite lean, lean but broad and solid. Beneath the black wool of his sweater she could see the movement of muscles, the tension in them and the slight hunch of his shoulders as he stood very close to the radiator, trying to thaw out. 'Mr Temple . . .'

'Are you still here, dammit?' He turned quickly, straightening to his full height of—what? Six-one, six-two? Whatever, Dawn found herself stepping away from him, caught herself feeling intimidated for some obscure reason—which annoyed her even more.

Her deep blue eyes went directly to his and she, too, drew herself up to her full height. No matter how he was feeling, there was no need for him to speak to her like this! 'Mr Temple, I'm afraid the . . .' And then she caught sight of herself in the wardrobe mirror.

One creamy cheek had somehow managed not to get dirty, while the rest of her face was quite grey with a thin film of soot. Her eyes were overly bright because she was angry, and her hair, normally so flattering to her, was sticking out at right-angles above one ear. With any other person at any other time, she might have laughed her head off. But not with this man, and not when she was so desperately tired. Rather, her appearance now came as a shock to her and it also served to wipe away all her confidence. Instead of putting the man in his place, she found herself almost bowing to him! 'I'm—I'll bring your drink straight away. I—er—will a sandwich be all right? Toasted, perhaps? Ham and cheese, cheese and tomato . . .?'

'Fine.' He waved her away. He sat heavily on the side of the bed and she was just about to close the door when he called her back—very sharply. 'Just a minute! Oh, for heaven's sake!' He looked thoroughly disgusted and Dawn hadn't the slightest idea what was upsetting him now.

'Mr Temple?'

'There's no 'phone in here!' Running long fingers through his thick, black curly hair, he demanded, 'Hell, *don't* tell me none of your rooms have 'phones in them?'

She didn't. She said simply, very quietly, 'There's a pay-'phone in the hall, just round the corner from the reception desk.'

Once outside his room, Dawn closed the door and leaned against the wall for a moment. She was seething but she told herself it was just her tiredness—and his. No doubt he would be human again in the morning. She certainly hoped so. Business might be bad at the moment but this was one guest she couldn't wait to get rid of.

By the time she got downstairs she was in a quandary. Should she take him a drink immediately? He was obviously desperate for one. Or should she take it up when she took his sandwich? She decided on the first idea—that was safest.

It simply wasn't worth opening the bar so she half-filled a glass with whisky from her mother's drinks cabinet in the living room. Only then did she realise quite how much the man had intimidated her. There was something about him which made her feel as though he *ought* to have the best and she felt almost guilty because there was no telephone in his room. This, while at the same time she would like nothing better than to give him a piece of her mind, to point out to him that for the prices he would pay here, he'd get very good value indeed.

One minute later she virtually marched up the stairs with his drink, the ambivalence of her thoughts in itself making her angrier. As she knocked on his door she told herself to calm down, to put things in perspective, because the top and bottom of it was that she was mentally and physically shattered and she just wasn't coping very well.

'Come.'

At the sound of his voice Dawn opened his bedroom door and put his drink on the bedside cabinet. Her facial expression did not change one iota, though a ripple of shock went unmistakably through her body. It was by no means the first time she'd seen a male guest in a state of undress. During her days at the inn, both recently and in the past, she had walked in on total strangers and found them sleeping in their beds or snoring in their beds or drunk in their beds. Everyone who has worked as a chambermaid has had the same experience and the absence of a reply when one knocks on a door is no guarantee that the bedroom is empty. People don't always make use of 'do not disturb' signs ... and a pass-key is a pass-key. So she shouldn't have been at all perturbed to find Mr Cosmo Temple naked from the waist up.

But she was.

Apart from throwing her a curt nod, he ignored her completely and was pulling off his shoes as Dawn put his drink down. She got out of the room as quickly as possible but there was more than enough time for her to acknowledge what an attractive man he was. Glancing down at him in profile she saw long, dark lashes casting a shadow on his lean face. The tan of his skin was as deep on his body as it was on his face, and his chest was covered with a mass of dark hair which went down to the taut muscles of his stomach and disappeared below the waistband of his slacks.

Again she was just about to close the door when he spoke to her. 'Hold that sandwich for ten minutes, will you? Give me time to take a bath. And could you possibly rustle up some hot soup? You must have something in a tin?'

'Yes. I—yes, of course.' Anything, anything, she just wanted to get out of there! But what on earth was she being so silly about? A half-naked man? So what?

She made her way to the kitchens and put a light under the remainder of the home-made soup she had served at dinner. Unable to understand her own reaction, her wish to look him over more thoroughly than she had, even while she'd felt vaguely embarrassed by the sight, she spent five minutes thinking about the man in room twelve. What was he? Who was he? Where was he heading tonight and where had he been? He'd certainly been more civil to her on their second encounter. Thank goodness she hadn't given him a piece of her mind; she'd been right all along in putting his initial rudeness down to exhaustion.

Or so she thought.

It was a physical effort for her to climb the stairs again but she did so fifteen minutes later. In her hands there was a tray set with piping hot soup and a toasted sandwich, on her face there was the smile which normally came very easily to her and required no effort at all.

The smile faded, however, when she went into his room again on hearing his one-word command. 'Come!'

With his long legs stretched out before him, the man was sprawled in the armchair by the radiator. In one hand was the glass of neat whisky and in the other was a cigarette. He wasn't even wearing slacks now, a white bath-towel was his only covering and it reached from his waist to his knees—just.

Dawn felt herself blushing from the base of her throat upwards but it wasn't caused by his appearance, it was the result of a swift surge of anger, anger which was becoming more and more difficult to suppress. He was shaking his head slowly, his eyes full of accusation, as though the breakdown of his car and everything else that was wrong with his world were *her* fault.

'Is something wrong?' She spoke crisply as she put down the tray. It was obvious that he hadn't bathed yet because the towel was bone-dry and so was he.

'One cannot bathe without soap—or maybe you wouldn't know about that. Tell me, are you the local scarecrow or do you actually have a function here? Are you chambermaid, bottle-washer, night-porter—or what?'

It was becoming quite difficult to breathe now, she was so angry. Summoning every ounce of her will-power, Dawn ignored his questions and got straight to his complaint. 'I'm sorry there's no soap in the bathroom. I'll get you some now.'

She was back in forty seconds, soap in hand. She'd done the quickest thing and had taken some from the vacant room next door. 'Now, if there's nothing else I can get for you, Mr Temple, I'll bid you good night . . .'

'You can give me some information.'

'Sorry?'

Very slowly, insolently, he looked her over from top to toe, his eyes reflecting all he was thinking. It wasn't pleasant. Dawn stiffened in resentment. 'Mr Temple, if you don't mind, I'm very tired. What is it you want to know?'

'Your name and your position here, for starters. You're not Welsh, your voice belies your ridiculous appearance and I'm interested to know what a girl like you is doing in a Godforsaken place like this. Then you can tell me exactly where I am, what's the nearest village within walking distance and what chance there is of getting my car out of a snowdrift near the forest a couple of miles back. You can then tell me how I'm supposed to find out what the weather forecast is when there's no television or radio in my room. After that, I'd like to know what time breakfast is served. And after that, dear girl, you may go.'

It was too much! It was too late, she was too tired and he was really too obnoxious to be tolerated any longer. Dawn put one hand on the door jamb, one hand on her hip and answered his barrage of questions in a voice which was drenched with sarcasm. 'My name is Dawn Davies. My mother is the proprietress here. I don't work here, I'm merely helping out because we're short-staffed, thanks to the 'flu epidemic. My mother and I are doing the best we can to keep our guests happy and comfortable. *Most* of them co-operate with us, *some* even sympathise, *all* of them are understanding.

'My mother is English, my father was Welsh. I was born in Wales, right here on these premises, so yes, I am Welsh, even if I don't sing my sentences. I look like the ... *local scarecrow* ... because I've been cleaning up a sootfall in the television room which is on the ground floor. The door has a sign on it, as all the common rooms do. You're too late to catch the weather forecast but allow me to oblige with the information: it's snow, snow and more snow.

'I have no idea who will get your car out of the snowdrift and I would advise you not to bank on it happening for several days. There are people in far worse situations than the one in which you find yourself, believe me. The nearest village is Betws-y-Coed, though Capel Curig, which is smaller, is fractionally closer from here. Since Land's End is technically within walking distance—given time—then the places I've just mentioned obviously are. How one would get there without a pair of skis, however, I cannot say. As for your breakfast, you can have that anytime between seven-thirty and nine-thirty, *in the dining room*. We don't provide room service here, Mr Temple, just as we don't equip the rooms with televisions, telephones or radios. But we do our best to oblige people and we don't charge a hundred pounds a night. In normal circumstances I'd remind you that in this life you pays your money and you takes your choice, but you've found yourself in unusual circumstances tonight. That, I'll grant you, but that's no reason for you to insult me and my home and the goodwill I've made every effort to show you. I trust that answers all your questions. Good night, Mr Temple.'

She stepped out of the room and closed the door quietly, but for several seconds she couldn't move. She was shaking from head to foot and there had been no satisfaction at all in what she'd just done. Halfway through her diatribe she had seen amusement creeping into his dark eyes, and by the time she'd finished, he'd been grinning. And now she could hear the low rumble of his laughter! *Damn* the man!

Why on earth had she allowed him to provoke her? It just wasn't like her to lose her temper. She should have kept quiet, because his amused response to her anger had made her feel even more furious.

CHAPTER THREE

THEY were snowed in and it came as a surprise to no one. Dawn was woken the following morning by her mother, cup of tea in hand, and the announcement that the snow was halfway up the front door of the inn. 'I've never seen anything like it! Well, not quite like it—and just listen to that wind!'

If it hadn't been such a worrying situation, Dawn would've thought her mother amused by it. Struggling into a sitting position, her mind alert but her tired body making a protest, she took the cup of tea gratefully. 'Heavens, it's six-thirty! Why didn't you wake me earlier?'

'Because everything's under control—apart from the weather. I've lit the fires and everything's ready to start cooking breakfast.' Shirley had had the benefit of an early night and she looked well on it. 'Besides, I'm told you were working till one o'clock last night—this morning.' She smiled and perched herself on Dawn's bed, her blue eyes lit with amusement. 'I'd like to hear your version of what happened with the man in room twelve.'

'Eh?'

'Mr Temple, the man in room twelve. You were running around after him, so he says.'

'You've—met him already?' Unpleasant, embarrassing memories came flooding back and Dawn surprised herself by feeling instantly cross. In the cold light of day, she found she could *not* forgive Cosmo Temple for his arrogance and rudeness. In fact the more she thought about the things he'd said, the angrier she

28

became. 'Obnoxious man!'

Her mother frowned. 'Obnoxious? I found him charming!' She shrugged. 'He was up before I was this morning. He'd been trying to get hold of the R.A.C. but they're constantly engaged. When I opened the front door to take a look at the weather, he agreed with me that he'd better give up on the idea of getting away from here. We're completely snowed in.'

'That'll please him."

'Well, he was frustrated, poor man. He said something about getting to Yorkshire and some business he had to deal with personally.'

'Tough.'

'Dear me! He really got on the wrong side of you, by the sound of it!'

'He was incredibly rude to me, Mother.'

'He's a paying guest, darling——'

'One we could do without. He'll be more trouble than he's worth. I lost my temper with him last night and gave him a piece of my mind. Not that it did any good—he seemed to think it highly comical——'

Shirley was bemused. 'You lost your temper? *You?* He didn't say anything about that . . .'

'I stood for a great deal of rudeness before I lost my cool, believe me.' Dawn sighed and flung the bedclothes back. 'How's Aunty Megan this morning?'

'She's still asleep. We're on our own again, I'm afraid.'

Within half an hour Dawn had showered, brushed her hair into its usual style and put on some light make-up. She took from her wardrobe a powder-blue woollen dress which clung lovingly to her figure then slipped into a pair of sensible, low-heeled shoes. Today would be just as hectic as yesterday had been and she'd be on her feet most of the time.

'Dawn?'

It was Miss Williams. She was always up with the lark and this morning she was hovering, for some reason, by the door of the residents' lounge.

'Good morning!' Dawn gave her a little wave as she approached her. Miss Williams was very prim and proper and she'd worn her hair the same way for as long as Dawn could remember. It was one of those permanently wavy styles which always appeared as though it had been kept in a hairnet overnight. The only difference these days was that it was greyer. In her middle sixties, Dawn's old school-teacher was just as buxom as ever, her back was ramrod straight and she smelled of violets. 'You've heard the news, Miss Williams? We're stranded, snowed in.'

'Well, that won't make much difference to me, will it, dear? Except that I won't be able to get to chapel on Sunday.'

Dawn suppressed a smile. 'It's only Friday today. We'll have to wait and see. Look, I really must go and help Mum. Forgive me, but I can't chat. I'll see you later——'

'There's something you ought to know, Dawn.' The old lady's voice took on a conspiratorial, disapproving tone, and she put a plump hand on Dawn's shoulder. 'That young couple who came yesterday morning, the pair in room five . . .'

'Yes?'

'They're not married! Oh, she wears a wedding ring, but they're not married, I'm sure of it!'

The younger woman kept the right amount of respect on her face but allowed herself a small shrug. 'I—it's really none of our business, Miss Williams. These days, people . . . what makes you think they're not married?'

'At dinner last night, I heard her asking him how

many sugars he takes in his coffee.' She gave a slight sniff. 'Well, it's obvious, isn't it? If they were married, she wouldn't need to ask!'

Dawn bit her cheeks and appeared to give the matter some thought. 'Maybe they're on their honeymoon? I mean, maybe they're not—sort of—*used* to each other yet.'

It sounded very lame and Miss Williams treated it with the contempt it deserved. She patted Dawn on the shoulder as though she were incapable of understanding such matters. 'I'll have a chat with you later, love.'

Chuckling, Dawn hadn't reached the end of the corridor before she was waylaid again.

'It's a bit much, Dawn!' It was Mr Hobday this time. Why was everyone up so early today? Of course, the Hobdays were supposed to leave this morning . . .

'Good morning, Mr Hobday. What's up?'

'What's up? I've been waiting to make a call and there's some bloody stranger out there who's hung on to the 'phone for over half an hour! Does he think he's the only one who's stranded? I've got to let people know I won't get back to Birmingham today . . .'

Dawn nodded sympathetically. 'Look, it's only ten past seven. Surely there's time to ring people after breakfast? No one will start worrying about you just yet. How's Douglas feeling today?'

'Oh, he's all right, just a bit of a cold.'

It worked. One customer nicely placated.

She heard Cosmo Temple's voice before she got to the reception area. The deep, low tones reached her before she rounded the corner and she paused, tensing. He was obviously still on the telephone and she could hear every word . . .

'There's no way I can get to Halifax, so you'll have to go. You'd better take a train. I'll ring Alex Mellor at his office after nine and explain what's happened . . . What? Yes, the business went well but I'm stranded in some cheap little boarding house in the middle of nowhere. Got stuck in a snowdrift. The car's okay, but what good is that? You wouldn't get a snowplough down the lanes around here . . .' There was a pause, then a sudden explosion: 'I don't want to hear about that, Richie! I've told you a hundred times before—women are *grief*!'

Dawn braced herself to walk past him, his words, 'cheap little boarding house' setting her teeth on edge. Unfortunately he hung up at that instant, his eyebrows going up in surprise when he turned and spotted her. 'We-ll,' he drawled, 'look at this!' The amusement she'd seen in his eyes the previous night was back in abundance. 'Good morning, Miss Davies!'

'Good morning, Mr Temple.' Dawn hardly looked at him. She kept on walking but he called her back.

'I'd like a word with you.'

She turned, hands on hips, facing him as though he were about to pick a fight. He was wearing a crisp, white shirt and a worsted, navy-blue business suit, and he looked very much out of place. He was out of place. He didn't belong here in this . . . *cheap little boarding house* . . . 'I have to serve breakfast.'

The corners of his mouth twitched and he leaned indolently against the wall, folding his arms across his broad chest. 'This won't take a minute.' He looked her over very slowly and this time there was approval in his eyes. 'You're obviously one of those women who look their loveliest first thing in the morning . . .'

'Mr Temple, you're wasting my time.'

'You have no time for compliments?'

'I have no time for sarcasm.'

'Except when you're dishing it out.' He smiled, was

clearly entertained if the laughter in his eyes was anything to go by. 'That was quite a speech you gave me last night. And, all things considered, I think an apology would be in order. Don't you?'

For an instant she was speechless. *'From whom?'*

'Why, from me, of course!' And with that, he stood erect then gave her an exaggerated bow. 'I beg to be forgiven for the harsh things I said to you. You were extremely helpful and obliging last night, and I do appreciate it.'

He just wasn't taking her seriously. He'd managed to apologise and to offend her further at the same time! A small sound of frustration escaped from her and she glared at him, showing all the dislike she felt for him. 'Another thing I have no time for, Mr Temple, is insincerity.'

'Insincerity?' The amusement vanished. 'I could spend fifteen minutes telling you how I felt last night, what a difficult and frustrating day I'd had.' He shrugged. 'But that wouldn't interest you in the least. I just hope you'll accept my apology.'

'I . . . ' She sighed openly, searching the dark, grey-black depths of his eyes in an effort to gauge what was going on in his mind. 'Yes, I accept it. Now if you'll excuse me.'

'Oh, there's just one more thing,' he said casually, and sure enough, when she turned to face him again, he was grinning.

'What now?' she demanded, cursing him silently.

'My laundry. I've left it on my bed. I'd be obliged if you'd get it back to me as quickly as possible.'

She was just about to tell him what she had wanted to say last night—that this was *not* the Ritz. She was about to say that here, in this cheap little boarding house, they did not do a laundry service. But he held up a hand as she opened her mouth, obviously having read her mind.

'I know all that, Miss Davies. But your mother said you would oblige. After all, I have only one change of clothes with me and I feel rather incongruous, dressed like this.'

'I see,' she said stiffly. 'So you'll expect your laundry to be done daily.'

''Fraid so. And who knows,' he added dramatically, his eyes flicking to the window by the front door, 'I could be here for weeks if this snow doesn't let up . . .'

She walked away from him to the sound of his quiet laughter. He'd been playing with her all along, baiting her. And he knew that she knew it. He was just waiting for her to lose her temper again. Well, she wouldn't. She wouldn't give him the satisfaction. She was not here for his entertainment!

'What on earth's the matter, Dawn? Why have you got that thunderous look on your face?' Shirley was eating her breakfast in the kitchen.

'It's him.'

'Who?'

'*Him.* The man in room twelve.' There was no point in telling her mother she shouldn't have agreed to do his washing. 'It's his attitude! I've never met *anyone* so arrogant, so sarcastic.'

'I really don't know what you're talking about! I told you, he was absolutely charming to me. Get your breakfast, darling, it's already on the plate.'

It got worse when Dawn put his breakfast in front of him. He walked into the dining room at twenty minutes past nine, after everyone else had finished, and ordered sausages, eggs, bacon and tomato. Shirley had cooked it to perfection but he looked down at the plate and said, 'Tell me, are you in danger of running out of bacon? I mean, being snowed in and all . . .'

'No.' Dawn spoke quietly, hovering by his table, just knowing there was something else coming. 'We've got enough food in the freezers to keep us going for weeks, if necessary. We might have to resort to powdered eggs and milk if——'

'Then I wonder why I'm being rationed? *Is* that streaky bacon—or is it a pattern on the plate?'

Dawn felt the hairs on the back of her neck prickling and it was with great difficulty that she kept her voice neutral. 'Breakfast doesn't live up to your expectations, Mr Temple?'

'Oh, it looks delicious, but really, two paper-thin slices! I mean, that's hardly enough for me to get the flavour of it, mm?'

'That's the portion we usually give and——'

'And you don't charge a hundred pounds a night here. I know, I know.' He looked up at her, his smile giving her a glimpse of white teeth which looked even nicer against the tan of his skin. 'For today, this will do, if you'll be good enough to bring me some extra toast. But tomorrow you must ask that good-looking mother of yours to cook me six slices. Put it on my bill as one of those little added extras.'

She would certainly do that! And the extra toast. And the laundry. And ten per cent service charge. And anything else she could think of.

'Six slices. His lordship wants *six* slices of bacon tomorrow.' In the privacy of the kitchen Dawn gave vent to the anger she wouldn't show their guest. 'Have you made a mental note of that, Mum?'

Shirley was laughing at her now. 'It's perfectly reasonable, Dawn. He's a big man and he wants a big breakfast. And why not? What *has* he done to upset you? It's not like you to react like this, I've never seen you so—what's the word they use these days? Uptight?'

'I've told you, it's just his attitude.'

'You'd better take him the extra toast he's asked for. Here you are.'

He asked for more coffee, too. Dawn placed it carefully in front of him and gave him her sweetest smile. She was proud of herself for that.

His eyebrows twitched in amusement. 'Ah, now that's what I like—service with a smile! It suits you. That frilly little apron suits you, too. What a helpful, domesticated woman you are, Miss Davies!'

He'd promoted her overnight, it seemed. The previous evening, he'd referred to her as 'girl'. Now she was a woman. She didn't answer him, didn't rise to the bait. Domesticated, indeed!

She was clearing the tables when next he spoke. 'That painting over there. Was it done by a local artist?'

Dawn's hands stilled momentarily as she was stacking a tray. If he insulted her work, something which was so close to her heart, she couldn't vouch for her reaction. Fair, constructive criticism was one thing, ribbing or laughter was quite another. The painting he was referring to was on the far wall and it was something she had done when she was fifteen. It was the view of the surrounding countryside, which she'd painted during the autumn, from an upstairs room.

She personally had not been satisfied with the painting, hadn't put her name to it, but her parents had loved it. It had stood in the dining room ever since. There were other, signed, paintings of hers here and there in various rooms of the inn, perhaps half a dozen of them, and they had all been done when she was in her middle teens, in what she now thought of as her dabbling stage, her experimental stage. In those days she had drawn and painted everything and anything, prior to her development, her training, her realisation that it was not painting but design and illustration that was her forte.

There were other paintings dotted about, too. There were several which had been done by a lady who lived in Betws-y-Coed, for whom the art was a hobby, though they were all for sale and they all had a tiny price label on them. Shirley took a small commission on any which were sold (visitors sometimes bought them, particularly landscapes) and the artist herself was grateful that her work was constantly on show. It was a common arrangement in hotels.

Cosmo Temple repeated his question and Dawn continued to stack the tray, not looking at him. 'Yes, it was done by a local artist.'

'But not the one whose painting is in reception.'

'No.'

'I can't see a signature from here. Or a price tag.'

She still didn't look at him. She picked up the tray and headed for the kitchen, feeling disproportionately tense. 'That one isn't for sale.'

'A pity. I like it very much indeed. It shows a lot of talent. Something which could be much improved on but it's very good, nevertheless.'

She just caught herself in time. She almost said thank you, but that would have led to more conversation and the sooner this man was out of her sight, the happier she'd be.

It was almost noon before he bothered her again. She was standing in reception, looking out of the window, taking two minutes all to herself before she got on with her next chore. She had collected the newcomer's washing while he was out of his room, cleaned up after him and made his bed. In fact she'd done all the bedrooms while her mother pressed on in the kitchens and the dining room, setting the tables and preparing lunch.

Dawn had also managed to spend five minutes with her aunt and with Bill and Wendy, the two staff who were also in bed with the 'flu. She took each of them a light omelette and a pot of tea, and was very gratified to hear the barman saying he felt considerably better today. He still looked washed out, though, and Dawn advised him to stay put, much as they could have used his help. Bill Madoc had lived and worked at the inn since Dawn's father had died, and nobody realised more than she that he would be up and working if he felt well enough.

A chat with Miss Williams was something Dawn hadn't managed but she promised herself she'd do so at tea-time. It had been, to say the least, a hectic morning.

By noon the wind had finally dropped, though the snow kept falling. There was a peculiar, unusual quietness outside which appealed to Dawn's fertile imagination as she stood, looking out, and gave her the feeling that this building was really the only place left on earth. Not a footprint, not a car-track, not a thing could be seen from the window. Everything was thickly coated in white and, at last, everything was still. There was no movement in the heavily laden trees, not even the sound of an aircraft shattered the silent stillness.

It was the door opening on to reception that broke her brief reverie, the door to the family's sitting room, and in the doorway stood Cosmo Temple. Startled, Dawn snapped at him. 'What the devil were you doing in our private sitting room?'

He just looked at her. 'Tell me, are you always this aggressive or have you got something against me?'

'Just answer my question.'

She saw his jaw tighten. He didn't like being spoken to like this, that was very obvious. Hard luck!

'Very well. I was using your private telephone. I had

several long distance telephone calls to make and I did
not wish to be interrupted by the noise coming from
those two teenagers and the television. Nor did I wish
to be overheard, this time, by anyone who happened to
be floating down the corridor. So I spoke with your
mother and——'

'Don't bother.' Dawn held up a hand. 'I can see it
coming. It's another of those little added extras, right?
And you told Mum to put it on your bill.'

He took two steps towards her and looked down at
her from his superior height. He dwarfed her by a good
nine inches and it made her, for some reason, suddenly
aware of her own femininity, her comparative smallness.
Feeling suddenly nervous, too, and at a loss to explain
it, she looked away from him, could no longer meet the
penetrating gaze of eyes which had grown cold.

But Cosmo Temple wasn't having that. He put one
long, lean finger under her chin and tilted her head up,
forcing her to look at him, even though his touch was
light. 'I am becoming,' he said quietly, patiently, 'just a
little bit bored with this. You either glare at me or you
won't look at me at all. Now listen. I've made my
apology, I've given you my explanation and I am not
going to repeat either of them. I am used to being
waited on, I'm used to being looked after and I'm used
to paying for that privilege.'

She couldn't move a muscle. Her face felt hot. He
was standing so close to her that his breath was a cool
fan against her skin, his words washing over her slowly
but steadily in that precise, attractive voice of his. He
was not putting her in her place, as she'd tried to do
with him last night, he was appealing to her common-
sense, somehow managing to make her feel it was *she*
who'd behaved unreasonably.

Had she? It was true that she didn't normally react to

people like this, didn't normally lose her self-control in any way. But there was something about him that brought out the worst in her, even when he was being civil, and she was damned if she could fathom quite what it was.

And he hadn't finished with her yet. 'I don't want to be here any more than you want me here. But we're stuck with each other's company, and that's that. So stop this nonsense, Dawn Davies, because as I say, you're beginning to make my imprisonment here even more boring. Now I want you to give me some writing paper and six envelopes. After lunch, you'll be delighted to hear, I shall be out of your way, I'll be in my room for the next few hours, catching up on my personal correspondence. With luck I'll be able to post my letters in two or three days' time, when I bid you goodbye and walk out of your life for ever. Now isn't that a happy thought?'

'I . . .' She stepped away from him, her hand going unconsciously to press against her chin, where he'd touched her. She could feel the blush on her cheeks, she felt flustered and she resented him for making her feel like this. Giving herself a mental shake, she squared her shoulders and spoke briskly. 'I'll get your writing paper.'

She stepped swiftly past him and went into the living room in search of some plain paper, not thinking for one moment that he'd follow her. But he did, she turned from the sideboard to find him standing just two paces away. Without a word of protest, she shoved several sheets of plain blue paper and six matching envelopes at him. 'I'll put it on your bill,' she said stiffly.

He ignored that. 'What's wrong with the paper you have in reception?'

'Why, Mr Temple . . .' She just couldn't resist it. 'Surely you wouldn't want to write your personal letters on that paper? Not when it has the name of a *cheap little boarding house* printed on it!'

For a moment he didn't seem to understand her. Then his eyes lit up and he laughed outrageously. 'Ah! So that's what's upset you! But my dear Miss Davies, there was nothing personal in that remark. Let's face it, this *is* a cheap little boarding house.'

With equal falseness she addressed him as he'd addressed her, brushing past him in an effort to get out of his sight. 'My dear Mr Temple, why don't you just go to hell!'

Everything happened so quickly then. She felt the bite of his fingers on her arm as he spun her round to face him. She had only the merest glimpse of his face, just a split second in which to register that she'd gone too far, that he was furious with her. And then his face was too close for her to see because his mouth came down on hers in a punishing kiss which knocked the breath from her lungs.

Humiliated beyond reason, she shoved the palms of her hands against his chest and pushed for all she was worth but he merely slipped his hands under her elbows, pulled them outwards and kept a firm grip on them. The result was that she almost toppled against him, her small, bra-less breasts making contact with the warm hardness of his chest. For the merest second their mouths lost contact and Dawn's lips parted as she gasped for air. Then he was kissing her again and she felt the firm probing of his tongue as he invaded her mouth with an intimacy which made something contract deep inside her. Shock waves spread out over her body and reached the tips of her toes, the tips of her breasts, her fingers.

Horrified, she pulled away from him with a violence which made her stagger, reaching out to the sideboard for support. When she ought to have been slapping his face, all she could do was stare at him in shocked confusion. 'I—why, why did you do that?'

He seemed totally unmoved, shrugged carelessly. 'Just to prove a point. I told you there was nothing personal in my remark about the inn. I find the proprietress charming, and her daughter—well, what can I say? Very ... kissable. I do hope I proved my point,' he added, moving one step closer to her.

'Yes!' She almost shouted the word, backing away. Then she turned in a flood of embarrassment and walked too quickly from the room, leaving him where he stood. Ridiculously close to tears, she headed for the kitchens and then paused in the middle of the empty dining room. She had to compose herself. How, *why* had she felt such a warm tingle of excitement when he'd kissed her, when he'd done it so roughly, setting out deliberately to humiliate her? *Had* that been his intention, in fact? Or had he really been proving his point? Of one thing she was sure: she didn't know how to handle him any more. She couldn't win with him. Whatever attitude she had adopted with him to date, he'd somehow managed always to put her down.

Perhaps, she thought, she should just be herself from now on.

She would. She would not allow him to get to her— or at her—in any way ever again. She would be herself and treat him just as she treated all the other guests. But not yet. She didn't want to have to face him just yet so she asked her mother to wait on the tables for lunch.

'Of course we can swap, darling, if that's what you want. But ... why? I know you cook well but you don't like it all that much.' Shirley was already taking off the white overall she had on. It didn't take much guessing to realise what was upsetting her daughter. 'Another tiff with the man in room twelve, is it?'

Dawn nodded but did not go into any details.

At three-thirty that afternoon Shirley built up the fire in the family's living room and sat wearily in an armchair. 'I've set the Hobday children to work.'

'Doing what?'

'Shifting the snow between the back door and the storage room. It's become treacherous trying to get to the freezers, so I asked the boys if they'd like to earn some pocket money. They're well wrapped up and their father approved the idea. They're getting bored. I do hope they can get away by Sunday, Mr Hobday's due in work on Monday and the boys are due to start school again.'

'It's in the lap of the gods, Mum.' Dawn hoped they would *all* be able to get away. 'But this can't go on forever, the thaw's bound to set in soon. Anyhow, it's stopped snowing, so that's something.' She got to her feet. She'd spent half an hour by the fire, alone, and she'd managed to dismiss the incident with Cosmo Temple . . . more or less. 'I'll make you some tea, Mum. I won't join you, though, because I promised Miss Williams a chat.'

'Don't bother making tea for me, darling. I'm going to take a nap while I've got the chance.'

Mr and Mrs Hobday and the couple from room five were in the TV room, watching some archaic film. There was little else to do. Miss Williams was in the residents' lounge, reading *Pride & Prejudice*, not for the first time, and she was alone but she seemed happy enough.

Dawn took a tray of tea and biscuits in and sat next

to her on the two-seater settee. 'There's an old film on telly—Bette Davies. I thought you'd be in there watching it.'

'Not when that awful Mr Hobday's in there. Every other word is a swear word, Dawn, and there's no call for it. I'll pour, love.' She picked up the pot, a note of accusation in her voice. 'You didn't tell me this morning that we had a new visitor. I hear from your mother that he arrived late last night. Of course I haven't spoken to him yet but I saw him at lunch—and a very handsome man he is, too. I must say it's very nice to see a gentleman dressed so well, wearing a suit in the dining room. I approve of that. Who is he? Where's he from?'

'Well, he's . . . not on holiday. He's a business man, as far as I can gather. He signed in as Cosmo Temple, from London.'

'Cosmo? How lovely! The name suits him, doesn't it?'

The question provoked an image of the man with hair as black as jet in tight, natural curls. A man with grey-black eyes, sometimes lit with amusement, or cold with irritation, or enigmatic when they were giving nothing away.

Before she could answer the question, Dawn found herself looking at him in reality. He walked into the lounge, tall and lean and as smart as a whip, his presence commanding attention with that proud, if not arrogant, tilt to his head. His tanned face broke into a smile when he saw the two women and he nodded towards the tea-tray. 'Just what I need, a nice cup of tea!' Then, embracing them both in his sweeping glance, 'May I join you, ladies?'

'We'd be delighted!' Miss Williams answered for them both and Dawn groaned inwardly. Of course she couldn't blame the old lady; at this time of year there was little enough to keep her entertained. A newcomer to whom she had taken a shine would keep her going for days.

Dawn made the introductions and went to get another cup for Mr Temple. By the time she came back, Miss Williams was calling him Cosmo and he was calling her Daphne. He had taken Dawn's seat on the settee and was chatting as though he'd known her old teacher for years.

Astonished, amused, sceptical, Dawn sat on an easy chair and watched the interplay. What the devil could he have in common with Miss Williams? But they were talking about books—which was right up the ex-teacher's street—and Cosmo broke off to include Dawn in the conversation. 'I came down here hunting for some reading matter,' he said, 'And Daphne's invited me to have a look through the books in her room. She assures me they're not,' he added, glancing at *Pride & Prejudice*, 'all romantic fiction.'

Dawn smiled politely.

'I'm glad you joined us, Cosmo,' Miss Williams poured his tea. 'I'd have liked to have chatted to you at lunch-time.'

'Then why didn't you? You must join me for dinner tonight.'

Miss Williams beamed at that ... And Dawn, well, Dawn smiled politely.

'Um, do you play Scrabble by any chance?' Miss Williams looked both doubtful and hopeful at the same time. She loved playing cards and Scrabble. 'Only, I thought if we're all stuck indoors for some days, you might like——'

'I'd love to,' he said. 'But you might be sorry you asked me.'

'Oh? Why is that?'

'Because I'm extremely good at it.'

Miss Williams was tickled pink. She laughed so much that Dawn couldn't help smiling. Now what the devil was he up to? Was he sending Daphne up, was he patronising her or was he sincere? She doubted the latter very much and it was this alone that made her stay in the room. Seeing their permanent resident content with someone to talk to, Dawn could have excused herself and taken a nap. But she didn't. She was intrigued. Very.

The two of them chatted easily and Dawn let them get on with it, saying nothing. She watched with fascination Miss Williams telling a perfect stranger about her career as a teacher, how she kept herself occupied in her retirement, how she had once been engaged to be married and that she'd been jilted.

She watched with equal fascination the way Cosmo Temple parried the questions put to him, answering yet revealing very little about himself except that he was a financial consultant.

'And are you married, Cosmo?'

He smiled and shook his head. 'I'm not the marrying kind, Daphne. I was never even lucky enough to be engaged.'

Dawn frowned without realising she was doing so. On hearing his first sentence she had thought he meant he rejected the idea of marriage. On hearing his second sentence, she wasn't sure. Then, seeing a fleeting look of ... satisfaction? ... cross Miss Williams' face, she came to the conclusion that his second remark had been an attempt at kindness.

At that point Dawn got up. 'Well, I think I'll leave you two to chat . . .'

'Must you go, Miss Davies?' In an old-fashioned display of courtesy Cosmo Temple got to his feet, too. 'I thought perhaps——' He broke off suddenly, his glance moving over Dawn's shoulder to a painting on the wall by the door. 'What a dark horse you are . . . the painting in the dining room, *you* did it!'

The painting by the door was one of Dawn's. It was signed and readable from where he stood. He looked at it and he looked back at her. 'It has the same touch. Unmistakable. Congratulations. I see you are a woman of many guises, many talents.'

'I——'

'But of course! Dawn's a very gifted artist!' Miss Williams interjected and Dawn knew she had to get out of there quickly. Miss Williams was as proud of Dawn's talents as Shirley was—but her ex-teacher was prone to exaggeration in this respect. 'Ever since she was a little girl, she's——'

'Miss Williams, forgive me but I must get on. And I'm sure Mr Temple doesn't want to hear about——'

'Ah, but Mr Temple does . . .'

'Don't go, Dawn,' Miss Williams urged. 'I've got my cards in my bag. Aren't you going to have a quick game with us? Er—you do play cards as well, Cosmo?'

Relieved, Dawn almost felt a physical difference when he took his eyes from her. Miss Williams *always* had her playing cards in her handbag—and she had never been so glad about that as she was right now. She only hoped that Cosmo played.

'I certainly do.' His eyes were dancing now as he turned to the old lady. 'But you might be sorry you asked me.'

Miss Williams rose to it willingly. She looked delighted. 'Oh? Why is that?'

'Because,' he said quietly, with a very serious expression which was belied by his eyes, 'I cheat.'

Dawn walked out of the room with a broad smile on her face and the idea in mind that maybe, just maybe, he wasn't such a hateful man after all . . .

CHAPTER FOUR

EVERYTHING showed signs of returning to normal the next day. Both Aunty Megan and Bill Madoc were up and about—Bill because he was feeling better, Aunty Megan because she was stubborn.

Dawn still had plenty to keep her occupied, doing the bedrooms and the fires and the cleaning, but it was an easier day than the ones she'd had of late. She should have been feeling tired, but she wasn't. Perhaps that was because the sun was shining. The sky was clear and a delicate shade of blue, but the sun had no real warmth in it and it made no impression on the snow. It was still freezing outside; it had been several degrees below freezing point during the clear, cloudless night, and by dusk it was getting colder by the minute.

Everyone gathered in the television room at six o'clock to see the weather forecast. There was a high pressure expected the next day over North Wales. Perhaps that would bring the thaw. In the bar, after dinner, the weather was the main topic of conversation. Dawn was on duty, giving her mother and her aunt the rest of the evening off. Bill had gone back to bed because he'd overdone things on his first day up. The young couple from room five were in, at a corner table where they chatted to the Hobdays, and all of them were frustrated and worrying because they had jobs to go to on Monday morning and no way of knowing whether they'd get away the next day, Sunday.

Neither Cosmo nor Miss Williams had been seen since dinner. They had shared a table again, as they had the night before and at lunch-time today, and Dawn assumed they were playing cards in the lounge. She certainly didn't expect Miss Williams to come into the public bar; that was not the way she liked to pass her time!

Cosmo came in, alone, at a little after ten. He sat on one of the high stools at the bar and asked Dawn for a Scotch. 'Well,' he said brightly, his eyes full of mischief. 'I've just spent a very pleasant evening in Daphne's room.'

'Indeed?' She couldn't help laughing.

'She's a very sweet lady.'

Dawn nodded. 'She's also easily shocked. I hope you were on your best behaviour.'

He put his hand on his heart and tried not to grin. 'I didn't lay a finger on her.'

'Mr Temple! You know very well what I meant! I keep waiting for you to say something that'll upset her.'

'She's not the only one who's easily shocked, is she?' There was a challenge in his voice. They were speaking over a distance of several feet because Dawn was standing by the till, sipping a tomato juice. She didn't want to move any closer to him, and he realised this. 'Would it make you feel too vulnerable if I asked you to call me Cosmo?'

'Vulnerable? I—don't know what you mean.'

He watched as she put her glass down, her arms folding in an attitude of mild indignation and defensiveness. Then his eyes moved slowly over her face, her slender and curvaceous figure. 'Ah, but you do, Dawn. You know exactly what I mean.'

She looked away, she stepped over to the sink beneath the bar and started washing glasses. *Why* did he have the ability to make her flustered? She felt so— so unsophisticated in comparison to him. He was perhaps ten, twelve, years her senior but there was about him a worldliness which far exceeded his years. Or maybe it was just that she lacked his experience. It was as if he knew, not suspected but *knew* what she had felt when he'd kissed her, and the thought of that was mortifying.

'Come here,' he said then. 'I want to talk to you.'

'Really, Cosmo, I can't chat. I've got several things to do before I close up.' She spoke lightly, deliberately using his first name as if she'd always done so. 'In fact, I'll give you another drink now because I must nip outside and get some food from the freezers.'

He didn't push it, he merely bowed his head in an attitude of acquiescence and thanked her when she put another Scotch in front of him.

She didn't have to go outside at all; what she'd suddenly remembered was his laundry. Shirley had done it, had ironed his belongings and left them neatly folded in the airing cupboards where all the bedding was kept, just as she had done the day before. What Dawn wanted to do now was to put it in his room while he was elsewhere. She didn't want to find herself alone with him again, not even for a moment.

He was wearing his slacks and his black cashmere sweater today; it was his shirt that she hung in his wardrobe, next to the navy suit. She left his pants and his socks on his bed, knowing a curious, unjustifiable feeling of intimacy in handling the garments. On the bedside table there was a pocket calculator, a pad full of scribbled figures, odd words which made no sense. Next to that were a couple of newspapers, days old, open on the crossword pages, and on top of the papers was a silver pen that looked as though it had cost the earth.

She gave a small tug on the bedspread, straightening it, and left the room feeling oddly like an intruder.

When she got back to the bar it was to find him sitting alone at a table. The Hobdays had gone and the couple from room five were just leaving. Good nights were exchanged, then she found herself alone with Cosmo.

He didn't speak, he just waited patiently until she'd cleared and wiped the tables, washed and dried the glasses ... and all the time she was aware of him, watching her in silence. It was only when she pulled down and locked the metal screens around the bar that he got up and walked over to her. 'Finished?'

She looked at him uncertainly. 'I—yes. I'll say good night.'

'Not so fast. I told you, I want to talk to you.'

'About what?'

'Your work.'

She was disappointed for some reason. She thought they had reached an understanding. Were things still not to his liking? Was he not being looked after well enough? She sighed openly, voicing her disappointment. 'We're doing our best, Cosmo. What is it you want to criticise now? Aunty Megan's cooking, my mother's ironing or my waitressing?'

He glanced around, waving her remarks away. 'Not this work, you idiot. I mean your real work, your profession.'

'Oh!' She didn't know what else to say.

He put a hand under her elbow and steered her out of the bar. 'Come on, let's make ourselves more comfortable.'

They were moving in the direction of the TV room but he halted at the sound coming from it. 'Damn. I thought everyone had gone to bed. Are your family still likely to be up?' He let go of her arm and again her hand went unconsciously to the spot he'd been touching.

'No. But I—I don't——'

Impatiently he told her to relax. 'I know it's not the most original line on record but all I want to see are your etchings.' And with that he took hold of her arm again and steered her in the direction of her mother's sitting room.

There was, she knew, no point in arguing with the man. He had the most curious way of getting people to do his bidding; even she had begun to serve him willingly, had found herself making certain his coffee was piping hot, his food presented in the nicest way.

She walked resignedly into the room and gestured for him to sit down. He chose the sofa; she took the chair by the dying fire. There were no games tonight, no teasing, no baiting. Cosmo lit one of his occasional cigarettes and got straight down to business. 'Yesterday I was treated by Miss Williams to a glowing account of your artistic talents, to a description of the day she first welcomed you as a newcomer to her primary school, and a blow by blow account of how you cried because you had lost your dinner money which had been carefully wrapped in a piece of paper and put into your little red shoulder bag.'

'I'm sorry about that!' She couldn't help it, laughter came bubbling out of her. 'It's your own fault for encouraging her!'

'I'm not complaining.' He wasn't smiling, either. 'Today I've been told where you've been working, how long for, and what you've been doing.'

Dawn had no idea where this conversation was heading, she was just enjoying it. 'So?'

'So what are you doing here? Why have you come home? You're not going to stay here, are you? You don't fit. I know this is where you were born and brought up but you're not going to spend your life here, wasting your talents, hiding yourself from the world.'

'No, I'm not.' She shrugged. 'I am looking for a job, actually. I came home for a few weeks, you know, to sort myself out and decide what I want to do.'

'And?'

'Well, I don't want to go back to work in London. Big cities and I don't get on very well. Not for more than a couple of weeks at a time, anyhow, not if I have to work in them.'

Cosmo was quiet for a moment, considering her. Not once did it occur to her that all this was none of his business. Rather she found herself waiting to see what he would say next. 'Have you thought of freelancing?'

'Yes. Well, the idea's occurred to me, put it that way. But I haven't done anything about it. Cosmo, why are you asking me all this?'

He didn't answer that one. 'May I see your portfolio? Would you mind?'

'Not at all. But why?'

'Just fetch it, will you?'

Every artist has a portfolio; he obviously took it for granted she had one. She dug it out from beneath her bed and handed it to him.

He spent twenty minutes, twenty silent minutes, looking at drawings, sketches, designs, myriad illustrations ranging from step-by-step cookery instructions to detailed sewing stitches to pictures of plants—the sort of stuff she'd been doing on the magazine. She waited patiently for his comments ... but there were none forthcoming. At length he put everything neatly away and astonished her by talking about printing, about colours, indeed getting fairly technical with her.

One hour and two drinks later, he got up, thanked her for her time and wished her good night.

Dawn stayed in the chair by the fire a while longer, bemused. She'd spent almost two hours with him and she had no idea what it had all been about. Furthermore, she'd enjoyed herself very much, had forgotten completely the very bad start to her relationship with him.

Relationship? What was she thinking about? She got up and automatically put the fireguard in place. In a day or two, if this high pressure forecast brought the thaw, he would, to use his own words, bid her goodbye and walk out of her life for ever.

She went to bed thinking that rather a pity.

Early on Sunday evening it started raining. Dawn had been given strict instructions by her mother that she was not to work, she was to take the evening off. Aunty Megan brought her dinner to her and she had it on a tray by the fire.

By the time Dawn had eaten it she was disinclined to move at all. Knowing that the pressure was off (the chambermaid was now up and about) she allowed the tiredness to take over and she dozed in the armchair. It was a two-hour doze and it was her mother who woke her, around nine-thirty.

Feeling very groggy, still half asleep, Dawn went straight to bed. She hadn't set eyes on Cosmo Temple since lunch-time, and he was on her mind as she climbed beneath the covers. Her dislike of him had dissolved completely. In fact, she admitted, she was intrigued by him.

'You're attracted by him, too, you ass.' She spoke aloud, adding to her honesty by putting the fact into words. 'You were attracted by him even when you loathed him.'

It was true. God, how complex human nature could be at times! To feel two such varying responses to a man! She switched off her bedside light, only to find that her mind had become too alert to allow her to sleep. It had been a mistake, taking such a long nap.

She got out of bed and fetched her drawing pad and pencils. Then she swapped the pencils for charcoal and began a sketch of the face of the man who was on her mind. Maybe, if she were satisfied with it, she would give it to him when he left tomorrow. Tomorrow was Monday; she could still hear the rain, pounding heavily now, so the prisoners of the Glendale Inn would be freed tomorrow, surely.

She worked until she'd finished the piece to her satisfaction. At midnight she finished another, similar piece, but this time it was a very detailed pencil drawing of Cosmo's strong, lean face. It was good, very good. She had captured his eyes in their enigmatic moments—telling nothing, showing only a fine intelligence. Maybe she would give them both to him. Maybe she would give him neither.

She got up, pulled on a blue cotton dressing gown and made her way to the kitchens. Maybe a cup of hot milk would make her sleepy.

The noise from the back of the building did not alarm her. It was probably just a cat. Burglars in this part of the world, in this weather, were not very likely. She pulled her gown more closely around her as she went to investigate and found the back door, by the kitchens, ajar. She flicked on the lights, was just about to close and lock the door when she heard the voice.

'Hey, hey, just a minute! Do you want me to get drowned?' Cosmo came walking towards her. He'd been standing several yards away, under the narrow shelter over the door to the storage room.

'Cosmo! What are you doing up at this hour? Why are you standing outside?'

'The same as you, I expect.' He stepped inside and

bolted the doors. 'Sorry if I startled you. I couldn't sleep, either. I was beginning to feel so damn claustrophobic, I just had to get out for an hour.'

'Horrible, isn't it?'

'The rain or feeling claustrophobic?'

'Both.'

'The rain's very, very welcome. I can't wait to get away from here, I've got to—— Oops, sorry! I've left myself wide open to one of your verbal attacks, mm?'

Dawn laughed and went to the fridge—only to be disappointed. 'Bother! This is the day we ran out of milk. I was going to offer you a nightcap.'

'Hot milk?' He looked disgusted. 'I'm thirty-six, not eighty-six. There's time enough for drinking hot milk when I'm in my dotage! Make that a brandy and you'll have a taker.'

Before she could answer him, he did it again. He took over the situation and caught hold of her hand, giving her a gentle pull in the direction of the sitting room. 'This is a stroke of luck, Dawn. I've been wanting to talk to you. I asked for you after dinner and was told you'd gone to bed, having crashed out in the chair and decided on an early night.'

'I had.' She was having qualms again, was becoming very dubious about being alone with him. For heaven's sake, it was midnight and what would her mother think of her taking him into the sitting room for a brandy, at this hour? And while she was in her nightclothes? Not a thing, probably! Shirley probably wouldn't bat an eyelid.

But Dawn needn't have worried. Whether or not he really thought her 'very kissable', he made no attempt to do anything about it. His attitude was one of detached friendliness and there wasn't even so much as a joke about her appearance in yet another of her 'guises'.

He accepted the brandy she handed him and seemed not to notice when their fingers made contact. But she did, and with the contact came a familiar ripple of shock. She took her seat by the fireplace, her hand going unconsciously to close the gaping neck of her dressing gown.

But Cosmo wasn't even looking at her. He spotted a pen and pad near the telephone and got up to fetch them, starting to write something as soon as he sat down again. Dawn watched in silence, intrigued. As he wrote, he said: 'This lady writes childrens' books. She's looking for someone to illustrate them. I think you could provide exactly what she wants.' He looked up then, the pen poised in mid-air. 'Assuming that sort of thing appeals to you?'

It did. Very much so. But Dawn was so taken aback she could do hardly more than nod. 'Furthermore,' he went on, 'I think you and she would get on very well together. I can't make any promises, of course. You'll have to go and talk to her.'

'Of course . . .' She wanted to bombard him with questions, but he was intent on what he was doing and she was still rather nonplussed. 'This—this is very kind of you and I——'

He looked up then. 'Kindness has nothing to do with it,' he said evenly. 'It's business. For you, for her.' And with that he closed the notepad, put it on the coffee table, picked up his drink and downed it in one swallow. Then he was on his feet. 'Unfortunately, you won't be able to see her until the start of February. She's abroad at the moment. She'll be back on the first of the month so ring her then and explain who you are. I will already have spoken to her about you by then.'

'I will. Thank-you. I must say, I never expected——'
Dawn stood up, following him as he moved towards the
door. He seemed determined not to linger tonight.

'Don't thank me.' He cut her off, turning as he
opened the door. 'Like I said, I can't promise anything.
Good night and goodbye, Dawn. And thank you for
everything.' Suddenly he stuck out his hand and took
hers in a brief, firm grip.

'Goodbye?' It wasn't at all what she'd meant to say.
'You're leaving—tomorrow?'

'Of course. First thing. I can dig my way out of the
snowdrift if necessary, though I doubt there'll be much
of it left by the morning.'

And then, as suddenly as he'd entered her life, he'd
gone.

Dawn was left, standing there, bemused, listening to
the sound of the pounding rain as it battered against
the windows, her mind filled with questions. Who was
the author he was putting her in contact with? Where
did the woman live? And why was Cosmo doing this?
He must have been very impressed with her portfolio—
but he'd said nothing. Nothing at all in praise or
criticism. There were only her paintings, he had
openly admired her paintings . . .

Yet she made no move to pick up the notepad. She
stayed where she was for several minutes, leaning
against the closed door and knowing a sense of
disappointment that after breakfast in the morning, she
wouldn't see Cosmo Temple again.

At length she shrugged. What of it? Knowing
him hadn't all been fun and intrigue, not by any
means. He could be an absolute swine when he chose to
be!

On that truthful note she shrugged again and crossed
the room to the coffee table. She flicked open the pad

on which he had written the telephone number, the address and name of ... Amelia Dunn!

Dawn's mouth fell open in astonishment.

Amelia Dunn, no less!

CHAPTER FIVE

'You know what they say, Dawn—don't look a gift-horse in the mouth.' The words came from Aunty Megan, who couldn't understand what her niece and her sister-in-law were fussing about. Aunty Megan, who was childless, had never heard of Amelia Dunn. She continued to stack the dishwasher, pleased but not ecstatic about Dawn's news.

'I'm not, I'm not! It's just that . . .' Frustrated, Dawn turned to her mother. 'Oh, isn't it annoying that I didn't get a chance to talk to him this morning!'

They were all in the kitchens, and breakfast was long since over with. Being thoughtful, Shirley had left her daughter to sleep for as long as she wanted that morning, seeing no reason to wake her early now they were fully staffed again. The result of this was that Dawn had missed her last opportunity to talk to, to ask questions of, Cosmo.

Shirley looked apologetic. 'He never said a word about this when he was paying his bill. Anyhow, as Megan says, just make the 'phone call in February and take it from there. Miss Dunn is obviously a friend of Cosmo's—otherwise he wouldn't be doing this. There's no mystery there. And he obviously intends to give you a glowing recommendation to her.' She looked at her daughter in amusement. 'I'm very glad you two got over your animosity. Who'd have thought you'd end up liking the man after the bad start you had!'

Dawn blinked at the statement. 'I—never said I like the man, Mum. I merely stopped disliking him, that's all.'

'I see.' Shirley frowned, curious, pausing for a moment. Then her face broke into a smile. 'Still, isn't this exciting!'

'Yes! But I—I daren't get too excited.'

'That's not like you, Dawn. What's happened to your optimism?'

'Nothing. But I have to be realistic as well as optimistic.' In the world of childrens' literature, Amelia Dunn was famous. She had been going for years; Dawn had read her work as a child, continuing to enjoy her books even when she was ten, eleven, twelve years old— by which time she should have outgrown them!

Amelia Dunn lived in the New Forest. But of course she did! Dawn smiled at the thought. Clearly Miss Dunn's surroundings were a great source of inspiration to her. Her characters, human and animal, all lived in fictitious woods. There was Simon the sly fox, Dolly Deer and Daisy the snail . . . Dawn remembered them all. She remembered also how beautifully illustrated those books had been, and still were, presumably. It had been years since she'd seen one.

'Mum?' She shoved her coffee cup away, getting quickly to her feet as she remembered her mother's tendency to hoard things. 'Did you by any chance keep my old books from when I was——'

'Yes, I did.' Shirley was laughing already, seeing what was coming.

Aunty Megan looked up from her task, smiling at them both. 'Have you ever known your mother throw out something which might come in "useful" one day?' The question came drily, despite her sing-song accent, provoking more laughter.

'They're in the loft, darling . . .'

Two hours later Dawn was still poring over the Amelia Dunn books she had read as a little girl. But this time she was concentrating more on the illustrations than the story!

By nightfall she had tried her hand at copying some of the illustrations, detail for detail. The result wasn't bad. In the morning, she decided, she would drive into Betws-y-Coed and buy some recent Amelia Dunn books. How much, over the years, would the style of illustrating have changed? If at all?

As the days passed, the idea of working for Miss Dunn became more and more appealing. It really would be a super assignment to land, this. Of course Dawn wasn't banking on anything, and she reminded herself that the author might be nothing like as sweet as her books were. She must be getting on in years, too— mustn't she? Actually, that wasn't necessarily so. She had, Dawn discovered, been writing children's books for over twenty years. Indeed she might be only as old as Shirley, who was in her middle forties.

By the last few days of January, however, some of Dawn's enthusiasm had waned. This was partially due to the lack of information which worried her. What sort of arrangement would Miss Dunn want? How many prospective illustrators had she seen—how many would she be seeing? And what had happened to the person who illustrated the last book? How many months' work would it entail? And how would she be paid, and how much? Most important of all: what chance did she have, actually, of getting the job?

When she made the telephone call to the author at the start of February, she asked none of these questions. She simply explained that Cosmo Temple had told her—and she didn't need to say any more. The mention of his name seemed to be enough.

'Ah, yes! It's Miss Davies, isn't it? I understand you live in Wales . . .' Amelia Dunn's voice was strong yet somehow gentle at the same time, and Dawn tried hard to conjure up a mental picture of the woman. The author's main concern seemed to be the distance Dawn would have to travel to see her in her home in the New Forest. Dawn assured her it was no problem, that she had a car and she loved driving. So the arrangements were made—though the date for the interview was fixed disappointingly ten days ahead.

Dawn put the 'phone down wishing that she could have seen Miss Dunn sooner. She was obviously a busy woman. Still, it was less than two more weeks she'd have to wait—and she couldn't suppress the resurgence of optimism that filled her. It would be so very nice to find a job she loved.

Once she had got past Fordingbridge, Dawn looked again at the directions Miss Dunn had given her over the telephone. They were getting more intricate now; she was looking for a sign for Godshill and the name brought a smile to her lips. Godshill. God's Hill? Was it a village or a small town, perhaps?

She drove on and when she actually entered the New Forest, she was enchanted. Several times she had to slow down from an already cautious speed to make way for the ponies who sauntered carelessly on to the roads, the ponies whose home this was. Now and then there was the sound, a short thrum, as the wheels of her car went over a cattle grid. She had passed through Godshill now and was getting deeper into the Forest. She paused by a heath to take another look at her directions, just loving her surroundings.

What a beautiful place to live! Not only because of the trees, the animals, the gentleness of the different forms of life around her but also because of the relative solitude, the privacy. It was mid-February and the sky was a clear, cold blue. The weather was still cold but there was something exhilarating about it today. And it didn't take much imagination to envisage what this place would look like when spring came, when everything was coaxed into new life and colour by that most inspiring of seasons ...

Spring. The idea suddenly brought a frown to Dawn's brows as she set the car in motion again. Spring was only four or six weeks away, and since the New Year she had done nothing at all about finding a job. Of course, she was on her way to an interview now, but she had let several weeks roll by whilst waiting for today, days when she should have been scanning the papers, 'phoning people, *doing* something. But, she promised herself, if she didn't get the job as illustrator for Amelia Dunn, she would definitely find something else within a month. She had to. She had been drifting aimlessly for far too long now.

Amelia Dunn's house was called Cornerways, for which there was no apparent reason, it being tucked into a shallow valley, and it was not in the least what Dawn expected. It was large and it was built of stone. It was also old—which was the only thing that fitted in with what she'd envisaged. But she had imagined Amelia Dunn to live in a rose-covered cottage, a small cottage that was painted white and had a welcoming trail of smoke coming from its chimneys when seen from a distance ...

She laughed at herself as she rang the doorbell. She was getting reality mixed up with fiction; the building she'd imagined was straight out of Amelia Dunn's books ... well, one of them!

The front door was made from solid oak and it was swung open by a woman who was probably in her early fifties. Dawn smiled and gave her name, thinking that this was not, this couldn't be, Miss Dunn. Not unless she made a habit of greeting strangers while wearing a gingham apron.

'Ah, yes. I'm Mrs Watt, Miss Dunn's housekeeper. Do come in, Miss Davies, we are expecting you.'

Nothing more was said. Dawn followed the housekeeper into a room which made her eyes widen in surprise. A new enchantment started here, right here!

Mrs Watt retreated, saying she'd tell Miss Dunn of Dawn's arrival, and Dawn looked around the room in amused fascination. There were so many photographs around! She couldn't bring herself to sit down, she felt compelled to wander around the large living room and let her eyes feast on the dozens upon dozens of photographs, most of which were old. There were sepia prints of people in uniform, people in wedding attire, people holding babies, people who—surely—were no more.

Yet Dawn didn't really *see* them, had no time in which she could actually absorb them, because there were other things which caught her attention. In the middle of February it was heartening to see so many roses; there were several crystal bowls of them dotted here and there on pieces of furniture, tables, pedestals, which were old but obviously much-loved, well cared-for. On the comfortably over-stuffed armchairs and the two settees were chair-back covers which had been intricately crocheted in the finest cottons. On the walls, which thankfully were decorated with a fairly plain, no-fuss paper, were paintings of various kinds. There were three portraits of people who no doubt were related to Miss Dunn, there were a couple of landscapes, one seascape (which seemed somehow incongruous) and several small, still-life paintings of various subjects.

There were also nine plants in the room, two of

which were huge. Dawn actually counted them, delighted by and curious at what she could see. There was no doubt in her mind, now, that Amelia Dunn was an old lady. This room was ... was full of memories. There was about it a feeling of ... time standing still. Encapsulated here was a time which was no more; days of gracious living, of beautiful clothes, of things of quality.

Dawn looked down at the intricate pattern woven into the old, square, Indian carpet which covered most of the floor. The floor itself was parquet, and where the carpet didn't reach it was covered here and there by small rugs which looked as old as the carpet, and as expensive.

She found herself sighing. This room could easily belong to someone who no longer had any money but who had been brought up, a long time ago, with a taste for fine things. If seen through the eyes of someone with a little less romance in her soul, or perhaps someone devoid of any artistry or imagination, Amelia Dunn's home might be thought to be ... shabby. Well, perhaps *almost* shabby. But Dawn couldn't see it that way. She thought it delightful, and more than anything else, more than the contents themselves, she was touched by the fact that everything in this room really meant something to its owner, was cherished by her.

Dawn sat down then, wondering what the old lady herself would look like, what she'd be wearing ... and a small smile tugged at her mouth. It was a smile which held not a lack of respect but a lot of understanding and just the tiniest hint of sympathy.

Amelia Dunn walked into the room as the smile was still lingering on Dawn's lips. It vanished immediately, was replaced by a soundless 'O' as the younger woman's eyebrows went up in astonishment. She couldn't help herself because Amelia Dunn was, and certainly was *not*, what she'd expected!

'Miss Davies, I'm so sorry to keep you . . .' She was small, a little shorter than Dawn, she was old and she was thin. And she was wearing a chunky, scarlet, polo-neck sweater and black corduroy jeans! Her hair was grey but it hinted here and there of the brunette she used to be, her features were small and delicate, and her eyes were a soft shade of brown which did nothing to detract from their liveliness, the interest reflected in them.

'How do you do, Miss Dunn?' As Dawn took the proffered hand, she noticed two things immediately. The old lady suffered from arthritis; her knuckles were swollen. It was the same with her left hand, too, on the third finger of which was a narrow, plain gold wedding ring . . . 'Oh, I'd thought——' Dawn caught herself in time before saying something tactless. 'It's *Mrs* Dunn, isn't it?'

'Technically, yes. I'm a widow.' The older woman waved her to a chair. 'But everybody calls me "Miss" Dunn. Or Amelia, of course. Why don't you start with that?'

Dawn was pleased, though for some reason she felt at the same time that it wasn't quite right, to call her Amelia, especially so soon after meeting her. 'Mr Temple said——'

'Oh, Cosmo's told me all about it, dear!' There was a wave of a hand, a twinkle of an eye which rather took the wind out of Dawn's sails. 'He told me what he'd said to you, about the work you showed him, about how he met you . . . and about the foul mood he was in. Mind you,' there was the wagging of a finger now, almost a warning . . . 'that's nothing unusual for him. My nephew demands a lot from life and from all who move in his orbit.'

'Your—*nephew*?' Dawn's surprises were not over for the day. 'He never said . . .'

Amelia Dunn merely shrugged, looking vaguely amused. Then the amusement vanished and she sat up, her small, arthritic hands moving in a gesture of impatience, though this was not reflected in her voice. 'It would be very nice, if we decide to work on the book together, if you would come and stay here, Dawn. What do you think? It makes sense, doesn't it? Obviously you'd have to follow my story and do the art-work accordingly and I see no sense in our sending reams of paper through the post when you're free to move in here. And Cosmo told me you are free to do that.'

It all seemed to come on one breath and she gave Dawn no chance to comment. Not yet. 'Of course you might not want to, and I'd understand that. You might have your reasons for wanting to stay in Wales. There again, you might not like the idea of living in a secluded place. You mightn't like the idea of living with a sixty-nine year old woman—and I shall be seventy in July! You might not like this house, come to think of it!'

By then Dawn was smiling broadly. The old lady's name came tripping from her lips as though she'd been friends with her for years. She was so very likeable! 'Amelia, I'd love to stay in this house! I've lived for most of my life in a place which is far more remote than this one. The idea of living in the New Forest appeals to me more than you could know. I am not, absolutely not, a city girl. Well, perhaps for a few days' shopping now and then!'

Forty minutes later they were sipping sherry and still chatting. Not a word had been said about business, not a mention had been made of Dawn's bulging portfolio, which was still in her car. On the contrary, Amelia Dunn seemed determined *not* to talk business, so Dawn followed her lead. She answered questions, occasional questions, but she volunteered much of what it was that Amelia wanted to know. And it was clear that she wanted to know whether she and Dawn would get on well together.

It was after lunch that they got down to business but it was Dawn who took the lead then. She had quite a long drive ahead of her and much as she enjoyed talking to the author, *someone* had to get to the point! After all, what if Amelia didn't care for Dawn's work? What if she didn't think it good enough?

She needn't have worried. She could, and she knew it, provide exactly what was wanted for the books. Amelia knew it, too. She had known it before she saw the portfolio; she had known it because Cosmo had told her so.

'Finances,' Amelia said at length. 'And my publishers. You realise you'll have to talk to them? Do you have an agent, Dawn?'

'Why, no. I——'

'Neither do I, as a matter of fact.' The old lady smiled. 'But then I have Cosmo to look after my interests, my money. Thank goodness.' Her eyes drifted to the window, unseeing, and suddenly it was as though she were talking to herself. 'I don't want ever to have to think about money again.' Then, very softly she added, 'Dear Cosmo. Dear, *dear* Cosmo.'

Dawn frowned in the momentary silence, which was broken by Amelia. She suggested they meet in London the following Monday to talk to the publishers, and Dawn willingly agreed. She suggested also that Dawn moved in with her on the Friday of the following week—and Dawn willingly agreed to that, too. She couldn't wait to get started.

'Now let me show you around.' Amelia got to her

feet. 'We'll start with the library, shall we, since that's where we'll be working?'

But Dawn didn't get to see the rest of the house, just the library, because it was while she and Amelia were in there that they were interrupted. Unlike the drawing room, the library was not at all eccentric. It was filled with books of all sizes and descriptions, fiction and non-fiction, and there was order about the room and no fuss apart from a few ornaments here and there.

As it happened, Dawn was standing just out of sight when someone poked their head round the door, so she was not immediately spotted. 'Amelia? Ah, there you are! Darling, there's no point asking us round for tea and then vanishing into your work!'

'Jeremy! Good heavens! Is it that time already?' Her eyes went apologetically to Dawn, which drew the man's attention to her.

'I'm so sorry . . .' he said, with an appreciative smile at Dawn, 'I didn't realise . . .'

Amelia crossed the room, holding her arms open to the tall, blond man as he bent to hug and kiss her. 'How very good it is to see you, Amelia. It's been too long. How long did you spend in Bermuda?'

'Three months. November to the end of January, as usual. You know I can't stand cold winters any more. Now let me introduce you to Dawn. She and I are going to work together.'

The introductions were made but Dawn already knew who the man was. She had seen him quite often on television; he was a very talented actor by the name of Jeremy Wright. Having read fairly recently an article about him, she knew also that he was divorced and he was forty years old—though he certainly didn't look it. He had straight, blond hair, laughing green eyes and an easy smile. He was the sort of man whom many women would find attractive, though he couldn't exactly be described as handsome.

When Amelia informed Dawn of his profession, she said, 'I know.'

'An out of work actor,' Jeremy amended, with another appreciative smile at Dawn.

She laughed, her blue eyes full of mischief. 'I thought you were supposed to describe it as "resting"? Besides, it won't be for long, will it? You start filming in Greece next month, don't you?'

'For a very small part,' he lamented. 'I get killed off in the first episode. I'll be back and out of work again within a few weeks.'

'Pessimist!'

Amelia was watching them both. 'He isn't really. He's just trying to provoke your sympathy!' And with that, she steered them both from the room. 'I take it your father's in the drawing room, Jeremy?'

'That's where I left him.'

Dawn made noises about getting on her way but Amelia urged her to stay. 'Just for a cup of tea. Half an hour or so? I'd like you to meet Major Wright, Jeremy's father. They're our neighbours, you see, and you'll be seeing quite a bit of them. How long are you down for?' she asked Jeremy.

'A week or two.' As they trooped into the drawing room he put a hand under Dawn's elbow, explaining, 'When I don't have to be in London, I make a bee-line for home—which is just a couple of miles from here. Dad lives alone and he likes the company. And I like to get away from it all.'

'You were brought up around here, were you?'

'Born and bred. Like Cosmo.' As Amelia greeted his father, Jeremy added, 'Have you met Cosmo?'

'It was Cosmo who put me in touch with Amelia,'

Dawn informed him, and he looked at her with a hint of surprise. She caught the look but she didn't understand it, and she found herself explaining more fully. 'After seeing my portfolio he told me about his aunt and what she was looking for.'

And then there was a hint of amusement in his eyes. Dawn wondered what on earth was going through his mind, especially when he added, 'Then all I can say is that you must be very talented.'

'Dawn, I'm so pleased for you, I just can't tell you!'

'I know, Mum. I'm rather pleased for myself—with myself!'

'And what is she like, this Amelia Dunn?'

It was late, and both Megan and Shirley should have been in bed by now, in view of the early start they made in the mornings. But neither of them could rest till Dawn got back, neither of them could wait till the morning to hear her news.

'She's lovely, Aunty Megan! She's getting on for seventy, she uses words like "ghastly" and "terribly", she's very English upper middle class, I suppose. And her *home* . . .!' Dawn happily gave her mother and her aunt a blow by blow account of her day. No doubt she would have to do the same for Miss Williams tomorrow. How she'd enjoy that! The news would keep her ex-teacher going for days . . .

'Fancy Cosmo not telling you Amelia Dunn's his aunt,' Shirley mused. 'Anyhow, I suppose that means you'll be seeing him sometime, at the house?'

'I'll be seeing him on Monday, actually.' Dawn spoke casually enough, but her mother seemed very pleased by the news. 'Amelia said we'll have lunch with him after we've been to her publishers. She said she always has a meal with Cosmo when she's in London.'

'You'll be able to thank him, then, for putting you in touch with Miss Dunn.'

'Yes.' Dawn tried to stifle a yawn. She realised that she was looking forward to seeing Cosmo Temple again but she wasn't going to say so. 'I intend to.'

CHAPTER SIX

THERE was a large, antique desk in her bedroom at
Cornerways. It was a beautiful piece and it was the only
thing in the room which wasn't modern. Unlike the
other rooms Dawn had seen, her bedroom and en suite
bathroom were very much of the mode of today. There
was an entire wall of fitted wardrobes and shelves, a
double divan with continental quilt, a TV, a comfortable, low-slung basket chair, and the suite in the
bathroom was pale yellow, with a complementary shade
of tiles, floor to ceiling. The carpets were plain and
there were no ornaments, no paintings, no photos, no
fuss.

Dawn was halfway through the process of making it
her room when Amelia knocked on the door. 'Gracious!
I came to offer to help you unpack—but I see you've
almost finished! What about that desk? We can have it
removed, if you like. George, that's the man who used
to live with me . . .' She smiled suddenly, realising what
she'd said. 'I mean, the man who used to work with me,
doing what you'll be doing . . . Where was I? Oh, yes,
George kept the desk in here because he sometimes
preferred to work alone. What do you think?'

'I'll keep it,' Dawn answered. Then, knowing Amelia
would not take offence, 'For just the same reason.'

With a look of approval, Amelia withdrew. 'I'll see
you at lunch. You probably want a nice hot soak in the
bath. After such an early start from Wales and all that
carrying you've been doing, you must be feeling stiff.'

Dawn wasn't feeling stiff but she was feeling grubby.

74

'A good idea. Er—may I ask—what happened to George? Had he worked with you for long?'

Amelia sighed. 'For years and years.'

Without realising it, Dawn found herself looking at the bed, convinced that George must have been as old as, or possibly older than, Amelia, and that he had died in the bed she was going to sleep in.

So when Amelia told her that George had got married and moved to Bournemouth, Dawn gurgled with laughter which was mainly aimed at herself. What an imagination she had!

Of course Amelia didn't see the joke, but she laughed nonetheless. 'My dear girl, what on earth is so funny? It seems you scorn the idea of marriage as much as my nephew does. Cosmo, I mean.'

Which seemed to imply there was another nephew. But it wasn't that which interested Dawn, she was interested to hear the remark about Cosmo's views on marriage. She had *thought* as much from something he'd said to Miss Williams, but she hadn't been sure. And hadn't she overheard him saying something scathing about women, over the telephone? Something about women being grief? It seemed an odd expression but that's what she thought she'd heard.

Their lunch with Cosmo had not taken place on the previous Monday. With apologies, Amelia had informed her that her nephew had had to go to New York at short notice. He didn't know when he would get back. So they had accepted instead an invitation to lunch with the publisher.

'Mind you,' Amelia went on now, 'I must say that we'd all thought George was the perennial bachelor. He got married on his sixtieth birthday, and I think that's rather sweet.'

'So do I,' Dawn said hastily, sincerely. 'I have

nothing at all against marriage.' She confessed, then, the thought that had flitted through her mind, and Amelia enjoyed it. She had, thankfully, a good sense of humour!

She was just about to leave the room when she turned, remembering something. 'By the way, I had a 'phone call from Cosmo this morning. He'd just got back to his flat. He's coming home tomorrow.'

He had just got back to his flat but he was coming home tomorrow? 'I'm sorry,' Dawn said, 'I don't quite understand. You mean he's coming back to England tomorrow?'

'No, no. He's in England now. He's at his flat in London at the moment. When I say he's coming home, I mean *here*.'

'Oh! This—this is home to him, is it?' Or was it just a figure of speech, the way a doting aunt might talk?

Amelia smiled. 'This *is* his home. This is *his* house, it belongs to him. He was born here and this is very much his home. Did he not mention that to you? If it were practical he'd be here all the time. But of course it isn't. He has his business to run and he needs to be in the city.'

After lunch, the two women took a stroll around the gardens, which were very beautiful and would soon be even more so. There was one acre of land attached to the house, and the lawns at the rear sloped gently towards a narrow stream. At the front of the house there were flower beds and a short, curving drive. Just a quarter of a mile down the lane, Dawn was told, were some stables where Cosmo kept a couple of horses.

Dawn was intensely curious about the situation with Cosmo and Amelia. It didn't feel right, thinking of this house as belonging to him, especially when it was so dominated by Amelia's personality, Amelia's things.

But it was his house. Perhaps he managed to spend very little time here? Perhaps he had been brought up here by Amelia? Was he coming tomorrow and staying just for the week end, or what?

She was curious also about Amelia; what had the author done with the first fifty years of her life? What had happened to her husband?

The questions remained unanswered because Dawn felt she couldn't ask such questions yet. Not yet. They were hardly relevant to work, and besides, it really was none of her business.

'I think I'll go inside now, if you don't mind.' Amelia touched her arm.

'Are you all right?'

'Yes, yes. I'm as fit as a fiddle really, apart from this wretched arthritis!' She gave a small shrug. 'I'm not a pretty young thing like you, Dawn. I feel the cold and the damp terribly these days. That's why I go abroad during the winter. I have a house in Bermuda, you know, and I would have stayed there for another month if I hadn't had commitments. Of course, Cosmo flew out to join me before Christmas, which was nice. I'd have got terribly bored had it not been for his visit. He stayed with me for two weeks. Believe me, that's the only thing that stops me from retiring and living permanently in the sun.'

'What? Cosmo?'

'Heavens, no! The *boredom*! The trouble is that I just can't write when I'm away from home. I've tried it; it doesn't work.' She gestured around her with the sweep of an arm. 'All Amelia Dunn's little people are here. Right here.'

Understanding, Dawn nodded. She let Amelia go back indoors and said she would see her later, that she wanted to walk farther. They had agreed that they wouldn't get down to work until next week, that Dawn should have a few days in which to get orientated.

Cosmo arrived at mid-morning on the Saturday. Dawn was having coffee with Amelia and they were in the drawing room, which overlooked the beautiful view at the back of the house. So she didn't hear or see his car. He was just, suddenly, there. He was wearing a white sweater, dark slacks, and his tall, lean frame filled the doorway as he paused momentarily to greet the women.

'Good morning, ladies. Not working today?'

'We're not starting till next week, darling.' Amelia got up to embrace him. 'Besides, you know I never work when you're here. I don't see you often enough as it is.'

For Dawn, nothing was quite the same, suddenly. The room, the house, the view, everything but Cosmo receded from her attention. She admitted she was glad to see him again—but she would not admit to there being a certain excitement in the air.

It was a minute or two before he came over to her, and when he did so he held out a hand. She was wearing a lilac trouser suit which did wonders for her figure, her complexion, and Cosmo looked at her hard, for a little longer than was necessary. And when his eyes fixed upon hers, she thought she saw a vague disapproval in the dark gaze.

It worried her, it made her feel uncomfortable, but a second later he was smiling. 'Hello, Dawn. Welcome to Cornerways. It seems everything is working out well, mm?' He cast a look in the direction of his aunt before adding, 'You've made yourself well and truly at home, I hope?'

'Very much so.' She let go of his hand, aware of Amelia watching the pair of them with a look of curiosity and interest on her face. As if to prove what she'd just said, Dawn went on. 'I'll just fetch another cup. You must be ready for a coffee. Mrs Watt's gone into the village to do a bit of shopping.'

She went into the kitchen, glad of a moment's privacy in which to collect herself. It had been ... something of a shock, seeing him again. It had been something of a shock to realise quite how much his presence pleased her.

Lunch and the entire afternoon passed very pleasantly without so much as a moment's lull in the conversation. There was news to catch up on. Dawn and Amelia told Cosmo of their visit to the publishers in London, of their long conversation on the day they'd met one another, and Cosmo spoke of New York, saying that he always enjoyed visiting the place but was always glad to get away from it, too.

He mentioned business as such only once, when he told his aunt how some shares of hers had zoomed in price during the past week. Amelia looked pleased but not impressed. 'Cosmo's a financial wizard, you know, Dawn.'

He jumped in quickly, grinning. 'You must allow for a certain bias.'

Dawn smiled, but Amelia dismissed his words with a wave of her hand. 'Oh, he's made his mistakes in the past, like everyone else. But he's also made a great deal of money for himself and a lot of other people. If ever you want advice, Cosmo's your man.'

With raised eyebrows and a tinkle of laughter she couldn't suppress, Dawn said, 'If I ever have any money to invest, I'll bear that in mind.'

Cosmo's eyes went directly to hers. With a somewhat sardonic smile, he queried, 'That I'm your man?'

Flustered because he seemed now to be laughing at

her, she shook her head and then nodded. 'I mean, I'll bear in mind that what you know about the stock market isn't worth—I mean what you *don't* know about the stock market isn't worth knowing!'

'I'm so glad you amended that!'

Amelia was chuckling. 'If you're anything like me, Dawn, high finance is beyond your ken.'

He went to bed shortly after dinner. He got to his feet and stretched slowly, lazily, and Dawn was unable to take her eyes from him. She felt suddenly aware of his strength, watching him, and she likened his movements to those of a sleek and powerful jungle animal. She felt this even more strongly as he walked to the door because he also had grace; he moved so easily, lightly, in spite of his height and size.

He was saying something about jet-lag and the various remedies that had been suggested to him over the years—all of which he condemned as spurious. 'There's only one thing to do and that's to sleep it off. Mind you, I'll probably be awake at the crack of . . . Dawn?'

There was laughter.

'Do you ride, by any chance?' he asked then.

She certainly did. As a youngster she had done a great deal of riding, pony trekking. She was nodding, smiling, hoping an invitation was forthcoming.

'Then how about it? Early tomorrow morning? Could you manage—say—seven o'clock? That's the best part of the day, you know.'

'I do know. And the answer's yes.' She wasn't even aware of Amelia's presence now. She was looking straight into the grey-black eyes and though there was some distance between her and Cosmo, Dawn saw nothing else. 'But you might be sorry you asked me,' she went on.

His frown was fleeting. Suddenly he was laughing, remembering the way he had teased Miss Williams that afternoon at the inn. He willingly fed Dawn the line she was waiting for. 'Oh? And why is that?'

'Because——' She changed her mind, her deep blue eyes mischievous as she decided not to give the answer he was expecting. 'Because I haven't ridden for years and I'm likely to fall off.'

At which Cosmo threw back his head and laughed as she had never heard him laugh before. It was loud and deep, rumbling, contagious laughter that made her feel almost stupidly happy.

And then he was gone.

She ran a finger along the roof of his car as they let themselves out at the front of the house the following morning. It was a navy blue Jensen and it was covered with the morning dew.

'Is this the car that was stuck in the snowdrift? Are we driving to the stables, by the way?'

'Certainly not!' He looked at her with disapproval but it was obviously a tease. 'It'll be daylight by the time we get there—if we walk slowly.'

At one point she actually had to ask him to slow down. He was walking quickly and she was having trouble keeping up with him. 'Cosmo! What's the hurry? I thought we were supposed to be *strolling*!'

He stopped instantly in his tracks, seeming suddenly, fleetingly, weary. 'Sorry. This always happens. I live at a break-neck pace in London and I always need a day in which to adjust when I come down here.' He took her arm and linked it through his. 'That isn't a complaint, by the way. I enjoy my life, what I do, very much. But I love it here, too.' With his free arm he made an expansive gesture. 'Isn't this glorious?'

It was. The sun was climbing higher in a cloudless sky. There was a chill in the air but Dawn didn't notice it. The birds were singing, everything was stirring slowly into life, the trees were moving in the breeze. But she hardly noticed those things, either. She was aware, too aware, of her arm linked in his, the physical contact, his nearness.

'You may take your pick.' They were standing in the stable and Dawn was looking at the two mares, gauging them.

She went over to them both, chatted to them, patted them. Then she turned to find Cosmo watching her with an odd intensity. 'I'll take the chestnut,' she announced.

'Thelma?' He smiled slowly. 'A good choice. Midnight can be a touch too—frivolous—at times!'

They were not the only people who liked to take an early morning ride on a Sunday, but it wasn't long before they were trotting briskly along the bridle path which led from the stables and Cosmo soon parted from it and cut a path through the trees. Dawn was right behind him, loving every minute of it. She had no doubt that he knew these woods like the back of his hand.

They stayed out for two hours and it was only when Dawn dismounted that she regretted this—as the stiffness set in! It had been a long ride and it had been a long time since she'd been on horseback. She grumbled to Cosmo, laughingly, as they each took a curry-comb and started to groom the horses.

'Ready for home?' He crossed over to her at length and took the curry-comb from her hand. 'I'm absolutely starving!'

'Me, too!' She looked up at him, laughing. Then she remembered her intention to thank him, privately and properly, for the favour he'd done her. 'Cosmo—about Amelia. It's so nice for me that——' She broke off, not wanting to make a speech of it. 'Well, it's so lovely here, the surroundings, the house, and Amelia is . . . oh, dear! All I want to do is to thank you . . .'

He smiled lazily, his dark eyes lit with amusement at her floundering, her seriousness. Then he put one arm on the partition, over her shoulder, and leaned closer to her, looking down at her with ever increasing amusement. 'Then why don't you?' Then he straightened to his full height.

Challenge! There was a challenge in his eyes now, in his stance, in his words, and Dawn cursed herself viciously for her stupidity. She was blushing! For heaven's sake, she was flustered and blushing like a schoolgirl!

It was an awkward, awful moment, a moment in which her mind raced furiously. She couldn't think of anything witty to say. Besides, if she made a fuss about this it would only make matters worse, make her seem more comical to him. So she took up the challenge and slipped her arms around his neck.

He didn't help, didn't respond. Indeed she had to stand on tiptoe in order to plant a kiss on his cheek. 'Damn you!' she said laughingly, glad there were only the horses to see her struggling to kiss him. She pulled away, her feet flat on the ground now as she grumbled to him. 'You didn't make that any easier by . . .'

She got no further. Suddenly the amusement left his eyes and he caught hold of her by the waist, drawing her body against his as he lowered his head and covered her mouth with his own. For just an instant she fought against this, wanting yet not wanting to be kissed like that. Not quite like that! Cosmo's effect on her was immediate and devastating . . . within seconds she was responding to him as she had never before responded to any man.

The kiss deepened and grew more and more intimate, more and more hungry. The more he kissed her, the more she wanted, and every inch of her body responded as his arms slid from her back to her waist ... Then his hands were on her hips, holding her firmly closer, making her aware of his own desire.

When at that point she should have pulled away, when in some confusion she realised that things were going too far, too fast, that she would never again be able to deny to herself or to him her desire for him, Dawn stayed right where she was. It seemed that her hands moved of their own volition and the next thing she knew, her fingers were caressing the short curls of his hair, his neck, and her body was moulding itself against his in an attempt to get closer, even closer.

But Cosmo Temple thrust her away from him as swiftly and as shockingly as he had taken hold of her. He almost shoved her away, half-turning from her, obviously angry for some reason.

Hurt, bewildered, Dawn had to reach out a hand to steady herself. She was staring at him in confusion, dismay ... and even before he spoke, she started to feel embarrassed.

'Well, well!' It was supposed to come out lightly but there was an unmistakable bite in his voice. He looked at her directly then, one dark eyebrow raised slightly. 'Who'd have thought it? Getting to know you becomes more and more interesting as time goes on.'

'I——what do you mean?' She didn't understand him. She knew only that she felt like crying.

He smiled then but it did nothing to make her feel better. 'I mean you're one of those women who look as though butter wouldn't melt ... Pretty little Dawn Davies,' he mused, 'with the golden curls and the big blue eyes. Such innocent eyes!'

Those innocent eyes had narrowed, were searching his almost desperately in an attempt to understand him. 'And?' she prompted. 'Go on, Cosmo, go on.'

'And nothing.' He shrugged, perfectly relaxed now.

Dawn was angry. He had not said anything with which she could exactly accuse him yet he had implied that she was not the sort of girl she seemed to be. 'For God's sake, anyone would think I'd shocked you. Or offended you. Or—or *something*! May I remind you that *you* started all that? It was not my idea to——'

'You may,' he cut in quietly. 'And may I make it clear that I'm not complaining? Come on, let's head for home.'

He reached for her arm but she drew away from him, almost hating him. He seemed to think . . . it was as if he thought that they'd have ended up making love right here in the stables if *he* hadn't called a halt!

She couldn't bear it. She couldn't bear that he might be making such an assumption. It was too ridiculous, too unfair, too vulgar of him! Yet what could she say? What, exactly, could she accuse him of? How much of this was in her own mind, not his? How much of this was born of her own guilt and embarrassment at the way she'd responded to him?

And she did feel guilty and embarrassed. He had managed to make her feel like that very easily in the way he'd thrust her from him, in the things he'd said. Her heart was beating rapidly as she followed him out of the stables, her anger and bewilderment making it impossible for her not to say anything further.

They had walked a hundred yards or so before she found the right thing to say, before she formed the words with which to defend herself against—well, she wasn't quite sure what. 'If for some obscure reason you're shocked or disappointed in me, I'd better remind you that I'm not a child. Nor am I a blonde and blue-eyed doll. I'm a woman and I am not made of stone.'

He kept on walking, responding merely with, 'I'm glad to hear that.' It seemed that the subject was closed as far as he was concerned.

For the rest of the day there was—or Dawn felt that there was—an atmosphere between them. If that were the case, Amelia certainly didn't notice it. Nor did he. Maybe it was all in Dawn's fertile imagination.

She felt relieved when he announced that he'd be leaving after dinner that evening. Amelia was disappointed; it seemed she had thought he would be staying for a few days. But Cosmo told her she'd misunderstood, that he had a meeting first thing Monday morning and he thought he'd mentioned that to her.

When she climbed into bed that night Dawn still felt troubled by what had happened between her and Cosmo, by the entire episode. What had he thought of her? What did he think of her? Why should she care so much? Because he was Amelia's nephew of course, and because she'd be seeing more of him and she wanted things to be pleasant between them.

It was only then, unable to sleep as she was, going over the incident and everything that had been said, that she realised how ambiguous her last words on the matter had been. In essence she had told him that if he hadn't expected such a passionate response, he shouldn't have kissed her the way he had.

She groaned and thumped the pillow in frustration. Is that what he'd understood from her words? She hoped not, because that wasn't what she had meant. What she really meant was that she had never responded to a man the way she had responded to him. But she could hardly have said *that*, could she?

'Damn it all,' she said at length, aloud, determined she would get to sleep. 'Let him think what he wants!'

CHAPTER SEVEN

'You're going home for Easter, aren't you, Dawn? When are you leaving? Friday, Saturday?'

'I think I'll go on Thursday.' She smiled over at Amelia, knowing this meant she had finished writing for the day. They had lived together for a month and had got to know each other very well. Amelia only worked during the morning—and she started chatting as soon as she'd run out of inspiration, or energy.

Dawn often continued working in the afternoon. But not always. Sometimes she'd go out for a walk, a drive to the village, with or without Amelia. Sometimes, like the older woman, she would take a nap in the afternoon. Life was very pleasant. Life was good. A routine had been established.

She had seen nothing of Cosmo, nor had she spoken to him.

He telephoned his aunt regularly but it was always Amelia or the housekeeper who answered the telephone. The only time Dawn answered it was during the mid-morning on Sundays, when her mother 'phoned.

'And when will you come back?' Amelia wanted to know.

'Tuesday, I think. Yes, Tuesday.' She spoke positively, realising that both the housekeeper and Amelia needed to know her plans.

'It will do you good, the break.' Amelia nodded approvingly. 'You've been getting just a tiny bit restless these past couple of days.'

'Have I?' Damn was surprised, amused. She wasn't conscious of having been restless.

'Just a little.' Soft brown eyes were watching her fondly. They had become more than co-workers, they had become firm friends. 'Much as I love your company, Dawn, I hope you'll never hesitate if you want to go out in the evenings.'

'But of course I wouldn't!'

'But you said no to Jeremy when he asked you out to dinner last week. Don't you like him?'

And so she had. She liked him well enough but she had declined. 'Yes, I found him very pleasant when I met him.'

Among other people, Major Wright, Jeremy's father, had visited Cornerways several times during the past month. Twice, both she and Amelia had been to dinner at his house, and Dawn had been flattered, touched, that she'd been included in his invitation. He was obviously fond of Amelia and a friend of many years. On neither occasion had Jeremy been there but he had telephoned last week, on his return from Greece, and said he was spending two or three weeks with his father and would she like to go out to dinner with him one evening. She couldn't really say why she'd refused the invitation and she worried, now, that it might have been unnecessarily rude. She hoped Amelia didn't think so. She hoped also that Amelia didn't question her further on the matter.

She didn't. She reverted instead to the subject of Easter. 'Anyhow, I'm glad you'll be back on Tuesday. Cosmo's coming down on Friday morning and I think he'll be here when you get back.'

Dawn was startled by her reaction to that. It made no sense at all, but it was what she felt. She felt sorry that she'd committed herself to going home for Easter.

She would rather have stayed here. If only she had known that Cosmo were coming . . .

Yet at the same time, a part of her was still annoyed with him. It didn't, it really did not, make sense. Nor did the fact that she thought about him often. She was too intrigued by the man, too interested in him for her own good.

'That's nice.' She had to say something to Amelia. 'He must have been busy not to have come home for the past month.'

'A month? Is it that long?' Amelia frowned. 'Good heavens, I didn't realise . . . Hasn't it gone quickly, Dawn?'

Jeremy rang again two days after that conversation, on the Wednesday before Good Friday. Mrs Watt called Dawn to the 'phone and she laughed at the way Jeremy greeted her.

'Good afternoon, Miss Dawn Davies! If you don't come out with me soon, you'll forget what I look like.'

'Hello, Jeremy. Now there's not much danger of that, is there? I saw you on the telly last night.'

'That,' he said dramatically, 'is not something I wish to be reminded of. It wasn't much of a part and I was not pleased with my performance. Now look, are you feeling any more sociable this week? I need cheering up . . .'

Dawn was amused. Did he think she could cheer him up? 'Oh, I'm sorry, I'll have to take a raincheck. Honestly, I simply can't. I'm leaving for Wales tomorrow——'

'So what's wrong with tonight?'

Nothing. She simply hadn't thought of it. But it was already turned six o'clock and—and why not go out? She had plenty of time in which to tell Mrs Watt she wasn't going to be home for dinner. Besides, it would make a pleasant change.

The date was fixed. Dawn plonked the receiver down and turned hurriedly, thinking she had not much time to bathe, change and make-up before Jeremy came for her. Her hasty movement resulted in her knocking a framed photograph off the telephone table. Of course, it would have to crash down on the parquet flooring instead of landing on carpet! She groaned, reaching for it, only to find that the glass was cracked. It was one of Amelia's favourites, too, the wedding photograph of her other nephew, Richie.

Dawn had yet to meet Richie and his wife. All she knew about them was that Richie worked for Cosmo, that he was eleven years younger than his brother, twenty-five, and his wife was the same age. Anthea was an ex-model, had given up her career when she married Richie eighteen months earlier.

Frowning, Dawn's eyes moved from the crack in the glass to the photograph itself. Unlike Cosmo, Richie was sandy-haired, good-looking but by no means as handsome as his brother. Anthea, on the other hand, was striking. It was easy to see why she had been a model; she was extremely beautiful.

The two of them looked so happy in their wedding photo but the one other thing Dawn knew about them was that their marriage was not a happy one. Amelia had told her this one afternoon when she identified for Dawn the people in some of the dozens of photographs which were in the room. Those were the words she'd used, their marriage was not a happy one. 'They think I'm not aware of it,' she had gone on, with a small, sad smile. 'These two. I think that's why they don't come to see me much. I suppose they think their bickering—and they do a great deal of that—would upset me. It would, of course, but I'd rather they visited just the same. I'm not a child who has to be protected from the facts of life! Besides, Cosmo has come right out with it. He said their marriage was doomed from the start. In fact, he said it before they even got to the altar!'

Had that been Cosmo's prejudice against marriage speaking or had he been far-seeing in this case? Dawn wondered about that as she put the photograph back on the table. She must tell Amelia what had happened and buy a new frame for it.

'My training in the theatre.' Jeremy said this by way of explanation when Dawn remarked on his punctuality just one hour later. 'One learns *not* to be late when there's a rehearsal or a show to be put on!'

She felt slightly awkward as she slipped into the passenger seat of his Audi. He was wearing an open-neck shirt, a casual corduroy jacket and jeans. 'Er——I feel I'm overdressed, Jeremy. Shall I change into something more casual?'

'You look fine,' he assured her, his eyes sliding over her with approval. She was wearing a simple shift in dusky pink with a matching jacket—but it seemed too much nonetheless. She had no idea what sort of place Jeremy was taking her to, but it clearly wasn't going to be glamorous.

'Relax,' he urged, slipping the gear lever into drive. 'I'm taking you to a nice, ordinary, country inn where anything goes as far as clothes are concerned. But the food! Ah! Now that's a different story ...'

Halfway through the evening Dawn decided that as far as dates with strangers go, this one was average. It was not particularly entertaining to be out with an actor, not when his main topic of conversation was himself. What made the evening average instead of boring was the unusualness, to her, of the content of some of his stories. She had had no idea what life was like behind the scenes in television—but now she had.

It was when the conversation became centred on Cosmo that the evening became really interesting for Dawn. And it wasn't she who brought up his name.

'I suppose Cosmo's been down a few times during the past month?' They were drinking coffee by then and Jeremy asked the question during a lull in their conversation.

'Actually, no. He—came on the first weekend I was here but we haven't seen him since.'

'Sounds curious, even ominous, that!' He had picked up her slight pause instantly.

'I'm told he's thinking of setting up a branch office in New York, so I expect he's been very busy.'

'He always is . . . with one thing or another . . . but that doesn't normally stop him from coming home, from seeing Amelia.'

It was Dawn's turn to pick up on his words. 'What do you mean, "With one thing or another"? It was the way you said it . . .'

He looked at her openly, innocently. 'Well, he leads a pretty full social life, doesn't he?'

'I wouldn't know.'

'Then take it from me.' He was grinning now. 'He has a weakness for beautiful women, and beautiful women have a weakness for him. The lucky dog! I've known him all his life, you know. We went to the same school, though we weren't in the same class. He's four years younger than I—again, the lucky dog!'

'Come on, Jeremy, you have no need to worry about your four years seniority. You're an attractive man, and well you know it!'

Indeed he did. He fancied himself, and then some. 'Then why don't I have Cosmo's pull with the ladies?' he went on. But Dawn wasn't going to flatter him any further. He was just fishing for compliments. 'Or is it that he has pots of money and I haven't? No, that's not the answer, because come to think of it, the girls used to make a bee-line for him when he was just a lad—a poor lad. I think that's why he's somewhat contemptuous of women; it's all too easy for him, attracting them.'

'Is he?' Dawn was surprised. 'Contemptuous of women? I'm told he's anti-marriage but I——'

'Ha!' Jeremy looked heavenward. 'That's why I was surprised at his having put you in contact with Amelia. I was surprised he'd put up with an attractive young woman living in his house full-time. Cosmo gets on just fine with children and old people—but women? He hasn't really much patience, he just loves 'em and leaves 'em.'

Dawn didn't want to hear any more. This conversation was disturbing her. She switched the subject back to Jeremy and his work—which was as easy as falling off a log—but she continued to think about Cosmo rather than listen to her companion. Was that why he'd shoved her away after kissing her? Because it had been oh, so easy for him to bring out that response in her? It was a depressing thought. She would make damn sure he never laid a finger on her again. She wasn't going to number among his scores of conquests!

It was only eleven-fifteen when they pulled up outside Cornerways, but the house was in darkness. Dawn got out of the car feeling enormously relieved that Jeremy made no attempt to kiss her. It would have been embarrassing because she certainly didn't want that routine. In fact, she warmed to him because he made no attempt even to give her a peck on the cheek.

She thanked him for a nice evening and went indoors, letting herself in quietly. She was crossing the hall to the stairs when the living room door opened and she

THE MAN IN ROOM 12

turned, startled. 'Cosmo!' For just an instant her pleasure at seeing him showed plainly. Then she remembered her irritation with him, an irritation which had been added to by the things Jeremy had said about him.

He was leaning against the door-jamb, his eyes narrowing as he saw her facial expression change. 'So that's how it is,' he said cryptically. 'Can we have a chat? How about a nightcap?'

'I—we weren't expecting you till Friday. I didn't see your car . . .'

He shrugged, smiling now. 'My car's in the garage and I gave myself tomorrow off. How about that drink?'

'No. I——' She didn't want to be alone with him. Nor did she want to be offhand, it would make life difficult. So she softened her refusal, feigning tiredness. 'Thanks, but no. I'm rather tired.'

Cosmo's smile changed to a knowing grin and he walked over to her, took her hand off the banister and took the decision out of her hands. 'After an evening with Jeremy Wright, I could understand that. However, you're lying. It's eleven-fifteen and a sweet young thing like you isn't likely to be too tired to have a drink.'

He was doing it again, taking over. And she was letting him. Again. 'Now,' he said, as she sat in the chair he led her to, 'I'm in no mood for heating up milk, so will a brandy suffice?'

Dawn nodded, laughing at the crack about hot milk in spite of herself. She took the drink he gave her and waited to find out what was on his mind.

He came straight out with it. 'What on earth did you accept a date with Jeremy for? Are you so bored here that you didn't mind spending an evening stroking someone's ego all night? Still, I suppose you'll have discovered that one evening with that old ego-maniac is enough for anyone. Did he spend the *entire* evening talking about himself—except for the time he took to tell you what a swine I am?'

At the look on Dawn's face, he started laughing. Her reactions to what he'd said were mixed. She was angry and amused at the same time. Either Jeremy and Cosmo were very good friends or they hated each other's guts! She put the question to him.

'Neither,' he said. 'I tolerate him and he tolerates me. He genuinely adores Amelia, which is one good point in his favour. And I put up with his occasional visits because I haven't given up hope that Amelia will marry his father. The old boy's proposed to her twice in the past year . . . and both Jeremy and I think it's an excellent idea. That's another thing we have in common, concern for the oldies.'

She would have smiled at his choice of word had it not been for her astonishment. 'You would encourage that marriage? Between Amelia and the Major?'

'Certainly.'

'But—but I've been told——'

'What? And by whom?'

'That you're anti-marriage. By everyone.'

'And so I am,' he shrugged. 'For myself. But I don't think everyone else should stay single!' He was laughing at the idea. 'What a boring world it would be!'

'And why should you be exempt? What have you got against it?'

His laughter faded, was replaced by a look of bitterness which puzzled Dawn enormously. '*I* like to be in control of my life. *I* and no one else. I like to be myself, always, without apology or compromise. And there's so much of that in marriage—compromise.'

'But of course there is!' Dawn was shocked. 'If you love someone very deeply——'

'I don't want ever to love someone so deeply that I'd change myself or my life for them. I've seen too much of it, Dawn, between people, bitterness developing, ambitions frustrated—how many happy marriages do you know of?'

'Cosmo, I don't know many married people.' She shifted to make herself more comfortable, kicked off her shoes and tucked her legs under her as she settled back in the chair. 'But I've seen for myself what marriage can do for people, and I mean the *positive* things. My parents, for instance . . .'

They talked for a long, long time. Dawn told him of her parents and their virtually idyllic marriage, and she was completely truthful. 'The sad thing is that my mother's family didn't want to know her when she married a Welsh, working-class inn-keeper. They spent a lot of time, she tells me, telling her she could do better. "Better". She came from a well-to-do family who thought it was very infra-dig for her to marry my father. How stupid can you get? What does it mean, "better"? How do you measure happiness? What was their yardstick? Money? Class? The presence or absence of an accent?'

But Cosmo didn't answer. He was looking at her intently, thoughtful, and their eyes held for a long moment. Then he smiled, a gentle smile. 'You're quite something, aren't you? How old are you, Dawn?'

'Twenty-three,' she answered, not seeing the relevance. 'Just.'

She thought he said 'So young', but he spoke so quietly that she couldn't be sure. Then he got to his feet, crossed over to her and took hold of her hands, pulling her to a standing position.

She stiffened slightly, shaking his hands away. 'Don't spoil it, Cosmo.'

'What? What do you mean?' He seemed genuinely puzzled.

'I mean don't touch me.' She looked up at him almost defiantly. 'I mean I've really enjoyed this evening—with you.' A hint of amusement touched her eyes as she thought of what he'd said about Jeremy—and he'd been absolutely right! 'Please don't spoil things now.'

He was frowning. 'My kissing you would spoil things, is that what you're saying?'

'That's precisely what I'm saying.'

He seemed highly amused at that. 'Well, I'm going to kiss you,' he said, reaching for her, 'and make a liar of you. I can think of no nicer way of saying good night.'

He simply didn't realise how serious Dawn was. She side-stepped him smartly—much to his further amusement. He seemed to think she was playing games and he closed in on her without haste, his fingers closing firmly on her arm, pulling her towards him.

'*Don't!*' The word came out very, very, angrily and her eyes were flashing dangerously.

'What the——' The grey-black eyes looked deeply into hers, and then they grew cold, narrowed. 'What the hell did Jeremy tell you about me tonight? What the hell have I done to offend you?'

'It has nothing to do with Jeremy,' she said evenly. 'Well, he did tell me about your—very busy social life. But that's none of my business. You're a free agent, you do what you like. But not with me, you don't.' She came out with it, that which had been bothering her for four weeks. 'That time in the stables, you—you insulted me. You hurt me. So just keep your hands to yourself from now on.'

'Dawn, what the devil are you talking about?' He looked as though he really didn't know what she meant, was staring at her in such a way that she almost backed down.

'You—you seemed to imply that I was—was some sort of—of vamp!'

Cosmo tried very hard not to smile. She saw him struggling against it. He put both of his hands on her shoulders, heavily, plonking them down in such a way that she could not misconstrue the action. Gently, he shook her, still fighting an amusement that was born of sheer delight. 'My dear girl, how wrong you are! How delightful you are! I wouldn't do anything to hurt you. Believe me, if I thought for one moment that you're anything other than what you are, you wouldn't be in this house now.'

'But you said——' She was indignant, she tried to shake him off.

'Now listen.' His hands closed firmly on her shoulders and he looked down at her with concern. 'No, better still—look.' With a gentle pull he led her towards the gilt-framed oval mirror on the far wall. He stood behind her, dwarfing her because she was minus her shoes, his hands still firmly on her shoulders.

She looked at herself, at him, in the mirror. 'Let me tell you what I can see,' he said quietly. 'I see a girl who is sometimes sixteen, sometimes a woman. I see a girl who has a certain wisdom in some respects and an enormous innocence in others. Some people are born old, Dawn, some never really grow up. I matured at the age of eleven, but for you the process is happening just now. This is why you quit your job in London and went home to sort yourself out. You're learning to be selective, discovering just what it is you want from life. You've acquired a veneer of sophistication but, thank God, it isn't enough to cover your honesty, your outspokenness, that very refreshing way your eyes

reflect your emotions, your anger, your bewilderment
... I remember precisely what I said to you in the
stables, Dawn, and I didn't mean to hurt or insult.
Rather I was echoing what was going through *your*
mind. I could sense it, see it, feel it, your shock, your
confusion. You just didn't know how to handle your
response to me.'

In the ensuing silence, they stood still, Dawn
absorbing all he'd said. He was right. Dear God, it was
as if he knew her almost as well as she knew herself!
'And why,' she ventured at length, 'why did you push
me away?'

Cosmo took several seconds to think about that.
'Because I too was shocked,' he admitted. 'I was
shocked at my own reaction.' In the mirror, his eyes
locked on to hers and he spoke very quietly. 'I wanted
you, I want you, more than I've wanted anyone in a
very long time.'

A chill touched her spine. A chill of excitement—
and fear. He was being honest; it was flattering, but
there was no way she wanted an affair with him. Until
tonight, she hadn't been wholly certain that she liked
him very much. Had she? 'I—there's nothing I can do
about that.'

This time he couldn't suppress his smile. He turned
her around to face him, looking down at her with dark
eyes which were dancing with laughter. 'You're not *that*
naïve, madam! Now take it easy, there's no need to
start blushing! Fortunately I'm acutely aware of the
difference in our ages, our—experience. You're no
vamp, Dawn. Believe me, I could never have made that
mistake about you! But you do want me. You know it,
I know it. But *I'm* not going to do anything about it.
I'm no cradle-snatcher, and you're not even sure
whether you like me on a personal level.'

He took his hands from her shoulders and stuck them in his trouser pockets. 'Perhaps you'll let me know when you've made up your mind. We'll take it from there, mm?'

And with that, he calmly left the room, calling over his shoulder. 'Turn off the lights and don't forget your shoes.'

She stood for ages, alone, dazed, trying to sort out what was happening to her, trying to sort out what she ought to be feeling. Indignation? Admiration? Anger? What—how was one supposed to react when a man said: let me know when you're ready to go to bed with me?

Was he the most arrogant creature on earth or was he simply a sophisticated, world-weary, experienced realist?

She ended up laughing.

By the time she got in bed she decided that there was no such thing as ought. What she ought to feel was what she *did* feel: fascination. He fascinated her. And if she were truthful she would admit that he always had.

She went over their entire conversation, from their discussion of marriage right through to the end. And she was left with one overriding question which she'd have given a lot to know the answer to: what had happened to him at the age of eleven? What was it that had made him 'mature' so young?

It must have been something very important.

And it must have had something to do with women. A woman. Dawn knew this instinctively. His mother? Amelia? What happened that had made him so dead set against sharing his life with someone?

CHAPTER EIGHT

DAWN apologised for the mishap with the photograph before breakfast the following morning. It was a beautiful day and both she and Amelia were up a little earlier than usual. Cosmo hadn't come downstairs yet.

'I didn't have a chance to tell you about it last night,' Dawn explained. 'I was dashing off to get ready for my date with Jeremy.' She picked up the photograph and took it over to where Amelia was sitting.

'And did you have a nice evening, dear?'

Dawn had to think about that if she were to give an honest answer. She grinned. 'Let's say it was—an unusual evening, all in all.'

Amelia chuckled. 'And you must have been surprised to find Cosmo here when you got back. I suppose he was still up when you came in?'

'He was, yes. We—had a nightcap together.' She sat down and showed her the broken photograph apologetically. 'I'll get a new frame while I'm away.'

'Please don't bother.' Amelia was unconcerned. 'I have several spare frames in my bedroom—of all shapes and sizes! Now don't worry about it!'

'Don't worry about what?' The voice from the doorway startled them both. It was Cosmo, as large as life and looking unutterably attractive, his freshly-washed hair looking even darker and curlier than ever.

'How did that happen?' He was standing behind the settee, leaning over to take the photo from Dawn's hands.

'I did it,' she said. 'I was . . . in a hurry and I knocked

102

it off the table.' The last few words came out very jerkily because the look on his face distracted her. He was studying the photo intently, as though he'd never seen it before. Amelia didn't see this; she had not turned round to look at Cosmo.

For long seconds he just looked at the people in the picture as though they were strangers to him.

'I look forward to meeting them.' Dawn felt obliged to say something. 'They're a handsome couple, aren't they? Anthea is beautiful.'

He didn't look up. 'Yes,' he said quietly. 'She certainly is. Very, very beautiful.'

There was something disturbing about that. Whether it was the unreadable look in his eyes, or something in his tone, she couldn't be sure. But it seemed as though it were an effort for him to take his eyes from the picture, and when he put it back on the table, he laid it face down. 'What a pity she married the wrong man.' He said it evenly, unemotionally, and Dawn found her eyes going to those of Amelia.

Amelia gave a small shrug, looking at Dawn as if to say, 'I told you so. He never approved.'

They all had breakfast in the morning room. The sun was streaming through the windows and Cosmo and Amelia were planning what to do with their day. Dawn had already packed her bag and had decided to leave for Wales before lunch. She didn't really want to go at all, not now Cosmo was here.

When she said something about making tracks, he looked up. 'Must you go, Dawn?'

His question pleased her. Their eyes held for several seconds, but she felt helpless. 'I—my mum's expecting me.'

'Yes, of course. Give her my regards, won't you?'

'Will you—will you be here when I get back on Tuesday?'

Her question pleased him, it was obvious from the way he smiled. 'As far as I know. With luck, I'll be here for the whole of next week.'

He was on her mind constantly as she drove to Wales. Moreover, he was on her mind all the time she was away. She kept telling herself that this was because she was obliged to talk about him so much, answering questions from her mother, her Aunty Megan, Miss Williams. It was only natural that they wanted to know about her life at Cornerways, about her work, about Amelia and the people they saw.

But it was more than that; Dawn missed Cosmo and when on the Tuesday she drove back to the New Forest, her excitement could not be denied. She was looking forward to seeing him so very much.

She was disappointed, however. Cosmo wasn't there.

It was mid-afternoon and it was raining heavily as she pulled up outside the house on the Tuesday. Mrs Watt's Mini wasn't around, nor was Cosmo's car, but Dawn assumed they were both in the garage. She let herself in at the back door, only to find the kitchen empty. Mrs Watt was out, the house was unusually quiet.

She had just stepped from the kitchen to the hall when suddenly the door to the drawing room was flung open and an anxious voice said, 'Anthea?'

It was Richie. Dawn recognised him immediately from the photograph. She smiled at the look of surprise on his face, a look which was fleetingly eclipsed by one of embarrassment as he muttered, 'I—I'm sorry, I thought you were . . .' There was a half-empty glass in his hand and he just stood there, looking awkward.

'Hello.' For some reason, Dawn felt instantly sorry for him. There was nothing of Cosmo in him, nothing at all. By comparison he was a boy, a boy who lacked confidence. Perhaps it was silly to feel this, considering he was older than she, but that was what she felt. 'You must be Richie.' She introduced herself.

He nodded as though he knew all about her. Then quite suddenly he flung out an arm, gesturing into the drawing room. 'Then come and have a drink with me, Pretty Dawn Davies, and you can tell me your whole life story.'

Only then did she register he was drunk. But how drunk? It was difficult to tell with a stranger. She looked at him more closely, seeing for the first time the pain in his eyes. What should she do? Where was Amelia, where was Cosmo?

Very lightly she said, 'I'd love a drink! Er—where's Amelia, Cosmo—everyone?'

Richie didn't ask her what she'd like; he walked rather unsteadily to the drinks cabinet and poured her a Scotch. She watched him, perturbed, calling a halt as he tipped the bottle. 'Whoa! That's enough, Richie! Put some soda in that, will you? Fill the glass up.'

He did as she asked and she said nothing when he topped up his own drink. He was drinking neat whisky and she wondered how many he'd had. He set the glass on a table beside her then flopped into an armchair. 'My aunt is taking a nap, the housekeeper wasn't here when I arrived, and Cosmo left an hour ago. Got called away, got a 'phone call and took off for London and the Temple financial empire.' He took a long swig of his drink and slumped forward a little, as though all the fight had gone out of him. 'Don't ever marry, Dawn. Take a word of advice from me: don't ever get married.'

She didn't really know what to say, how to handle him. 'Er—when did you get here, Ritchie?'

'This morning,' he said sullenly. 'When my wife announced that she'd had a 'phone call from her family, that her mother was ill and she was going to Warwickshire for the day. Which of *course*,' he said bitterly, sarcastically, 'means she'll be away for the night. *That's* when I left London, pretty lady, to seek solace here in the company of my gentle aunt. And Cosmo. And you.' He saluted her with his glass, tipped it back and downed the large drink he'd given himself.

Dawn looked down at her hands, pitying him. It was obvious that he thought Anthea had lied to him about her mother being ill. It was something he could easily have checked up on but he hadn't bothered. And he had obviously thought Anthea might change her mind about going away for the night—which was why he'd greeted Dawn with his wife's name. Very quietly she said, 'You're very much in love with Anthea, aren't you?'

He flung his head back, having difficulty focusing on her. 'Yes, I am . . . God help me!'

Feeling extremely awkward, Dawn wished fervently that Cosmo hadn't had to leave. He would know how to handle this. If Richie needed to talk, she was willing to listen. On the other hand, she didn't want to appear to be prying. Softly she said, 'Do you—do you want to talk about it, Richie?'

Looking almost like a stubborn little boy, he shook his head. 'About my wife's affair? I've talked till I'm blue in the face, to Cosmo.' He saluted again, his empty glass waving about in the air. 'To Cosmo. He warned me, you know. Warned me about her. And he should know, he knew Anthea before I did and he knows women inside out. He looks after me, you know, Dawn. My half-brother, my big brother.'

'Your half-brother? I didn't realise——'

'That we had different mothers? Oh, yes . . .' He was slurring his words now. 'We're not entirely of the same stock. The bad——' He got surprisingly quickly to his feet but he half staggered across the room, in the direction of the drinks cabinet.

'Richie, please, I——' Dawn bit her lip. What should she *do*? She didn't want Amelia to see him like this; it would upset her terribly. She guessed that Richie had hit the bottle when Cosmo left, which meant he'd been drinking solidly for an hour. But what right had she to tell him not to drink any more?

'What?' He turned to her, whisky in hand. 'Please Richie what?'

Taking the bull by the horns, taking a gamble, she got up and walked over to him, took the bottle from his hand and put it down. 'Don't drink any more. Your troubles will still be there when you've sobered up. It'll solve nothing.'

He looked at her helplessly, compliant, again seeming far younger than his years. 'Then what should I do?'

'Go to bed.'

'Now?'

'Now.'

He let her lead him from the room, by the hand, and she delivered him to the door of a guest room—the one farthest from Amelia's room.

Cosmo telephoned that evening. It was Richie he asked for. Dawn took the telephone from Mrs Watt, who fortunately had had the day off. 'Cosmo? It's me.' She told him of the state his brother had been in, that fortunately Amelia hadn't witnessed it.

'Hell, I'm sorry to lumber you with that.' Cosmo apologised and thanked her, complimented her on the way she'd handled the situation. 'What's he doing now? Still sleeping it off?'

'Yes.'

'Okay, leave him. He'll be different again when he

wakes up, like a lamb, you'll see. Look, I have to go out now, Dawn, but I want you to give him a message when he wakes up. Tell him very firmly that I said I want him in the office at nine tomorrow morning. Tell him I need him, he has work to do. All right?'

'All right. But I doubt he'll be in any fit state to drive tonight . . .'

'He won't need to. Tell him to leave there early in the morning.'

'I'll do that. 'Bye, Cosmo.'

'Not so fast!' There was a hint of amusement in his voice now. 'I'll be home on Friday. You have a dinner date with *me*—so don't let me catch you out with that gossiping Jeremy Wright again.'

Dawn gently replaced the receiver, smiling idiotically. Everything had been worthwhile, the trauma of the afternoon with Richie, everything. Knowing that Cosmo would be here on Friday put the sparkle back into her eyes and into her life.

Amelia was dining at the Major's house, Dawn was sharing with Cosmo a corner table in an intimate, expensive restaurant just outside Sandleheath. He had told her to dress for the occasion and she was wearing a black, low-cut jersey dress which was sophisticated in its very simplicity. Cosmo was wearing an immaculate, dark grey suit, a crisp white shirt and an air of total relaxation.

Even when he spoke about Richie, he seemed happy enough. 'He's calmed down a bit during the week. Hard work can be a marvellous balm sometimes.'

'And you're seeing to it that he's getting plenty of that?'

'Indeed I am. He'll sort himself out in time.'

'With your help, Cosmo.'

He shrugged. 'Richie is a very clever young man, believe it or not, extremely clever, and I'm not going to watch him destroy himself for the love of a woman. He's been hitting the bottle hard of late but fortunately his work hasn't been affected, not so far . . .' A shadow crossed his face, and Dawn wondered fleetingly what Richie's wife was like, what sort of person she was. '. . . And work is the only thing that keeps his mind off Anthea,' Cosmo went on. 'So I intend to delegate as much as I can to him, and I'll let him do some of the travelling I would normally do—where possible.'

He smiled then, reaching for her hand. 'Now let's talk about tomorrow and what we're going to do with our day. But first let me tell you how beautiful you're looking this evening . . .' His eyes moved appreciatively over her face, her hair, then trailed downwards to the low-cut neckline of her dress. 'You make it very hard for me to remember I've left the ball in your court, Dawn . . .'

She didn't take him seriously because the words had been said with a roguish smile. But they had an understanding, didn't they? And she expected him to keep to it. Nevertheless, she couldn't deny it was constantly present, this attraction between them . . .

It was a marvellous weekend, as was the following one and the one after that. Every Friday or sometimes Thursday evening during the next few weeks, Cosmo came home to Cornerways, leaving early Monday morning, leaving Dawn to spend the next few days with happy memories and a sense of anticipation.

They went out to dinner often, alone, they went riding together, they went exploring in the woods. Sometimes their conversations were intense, especially if they were discussing politics, sometimes they just fooled around and joked and laughed. Sometimes they took

Amelia out for a drive or to Fordingbridge to do some shopping.

With a sense of inevitability, and a sense of doom, Dawn was obliged to acknowledge what was happening to her. She was falling in love with Cosmo. He was— was so *good* to be with. Whether he were being serious or jocular or teasing, it didn't matter. She loved all these sides of him.

In the middle of May, one evening after Amelia had gone to bed, he told Dawn of the party he was planning for his aunt's seventieth birthday in July.

They had dined at home that evening, were sitting in the drawing room which was lit only by the light of the lamps. The fire had almost faded, the room was warm and cosy and the house and everything outside was quiet. The room took on a conspiratorial atmosphere as Cosmo told her he wanted to keep the party a secret until the last minute. 'She'd probably protest if we tell her what I've got planned. You know she's basically shy, avoids the limelight if possible. But there'll be no one at the party who doesn't love her. And that's not difficult for anyone to do, is it?'

Dawn smiled gently as he sat beside her on the settee, handing her a drink. She was touched. Cosmo Temple was not incapable of loving. He loved his aunt very much indeed, that was obvious enough, had always been obvious to Dawn.

'I've booked reception rooms at the Dorchester,' he went on. 'It'll be a glittering affair—the best of everything.' With a twinkle in his eye, he added, 'I'm telling you about it now because you'll want to start planning what to wear. For parties such as this, all women like two months' notice in which to do their shopping!'

That was the trouble. He knew women too well—to the extent that they'd lost their enchantment for him. She listened in silence as he talked about the party and the people he'd invited, loving him and knowing it was hopeless.

'It's very sweet of you to do this,' she said at length. 'Amelia's very, very dear to you, isn't she? I think it's——'

He turned to look directly into her eyes, his expression serious. 'It's nothing,' he said quietly. 'Absolutely nothing compared to all she's done for me in the past.'

It was at that instant that Dawn forgot herself, forgot her promises to herself, forgot about the dangers of ... She had only to put out an arm to make contact with him, and she did, her face uptilted as she put an arm around him. Then she was kissing him.

And then she was being kissed, being kissed as she'd never been kissed before, not even by him. It was nothing like the first time he'd kissed her, nor the second. It was utterly intoxicating because it was so long overdue. They were hungry for one another after all these weeks of—of keeping to promises, of keeping a physical distance.

But it had been there constantly for both of them, a desire of which they had both been aware, a desire about which nothing at all had been said for so long a time.

He kissed her gently at first but it rapidly grew more demanding, and Dawn met that demand, created her own demand as her lips parted to invite the exploration of his tongue. It seemed endless, feverish, as they clung together, moaning softly as their excitement mounted. Dawn made no objection when he slipped her dress straps from her shoulders, when his hands moved caressingly over her small, pert breasts, though in her head there were warning bells clanging. Even so, she tried to ignore them; this was too sweet, too *right* to call a halt to.

'Dawn . . .' Cosmo's lips were at her throat, burning a trail of fire along her skin, creating an awful, yawning ache inside her as she clung to him, loving him, wanting him as she had never wanted, never had, any other man.

And he was murmuring, all the time he was murmuring now, telling her how much he wanted her, needed her. 'Come upstairs, darling. Come——' Yet he didn't move away. Instead he slid his fingers into her hair, eased her back on the settee. It was when his lips closed over the tips of her breasts that Dawn came shockingly to her senses. She gasped from the sheer pleasure of the contact, aware that if she didn't call a halt now, she never would.

'Cosmo!' Very firmly she pushed him away, and he was muttering incoherently as he reached for her again, his half-closed eyes making her realise she had already gone too far. 'Don't, Cosmo! I can't—I haven't—I won't——'

It registered with him slowly, what she was saying. Then he pulled away swiftly, angrily, swearing under his breath. '. . . For God's sake, Dawn . . .'

'I'm sorry!' She held up both hands, defenceless. It was she who had taken the initiative, she hadn't forgotten that. 'I am sorry, Cosmo.'

She closed her eyes because she couldn't look at him. He was furious—and could she blame him?

There was a silence, an awful silence which stretched over long seconds. She heard a long, shuddering sigh which she interpreted as impatience, his displeasure. But Cosmo was merely pulling himself together.

Quietly, gently, he said: 'Go to bed, Dawn. Dammit, go to bed now before I change my mind and walk up those stairs with you.'

She didn't argue. She didn't realise either that the speed with which she got to her feet was laughable, that she looked to him in that moment like a naughty child who was being sent to her room.

But Cosmo couldn't smile. He was too tense even to do that as he watched her walk to the door, this girl-woman-child who fascinated him, who had the power to excite him beyond description.

At the door, she turned, throwing a quick, uncertain look in his direction. He smiled then. He smiled at the look on her face, he smiled because he just couldn't help himself.

Relief flooded over her. She watched the familiar, lazy smile change his entire countenance and she knew it meant that everything was all right again between them. He had forgiven her. They were not lovers but they were, at least, very good friends.

CHAPTER NINE

'WHAT is it, Dawn? What's wrong?' Amelia asked the question because she couldn't stop herself, not any longer. She had been watching Dawn for several days now, watching her grow just a little less effervescent, even seeming troubled on occasions.

While they worked, Amelia had watched her. Dawn's artistry was not affected in the least by what troubled her; on the contrary, it was brilliant, not that their progress mattered much. The book had to be submitted by the end of June, and it would be ready.

For the past few years Amelia had worked at a slower pace than she used to, and she had only one more book to write, after this one, to fulfil her current contract with her publishers. She had mentioned this to Dawn—what she hadn't mentioned was that she was seriously considering the Major's proposal of marriage, that she was thinking of retiring altogether.

Dawn looked up from her work. There were so many questions she wanted to ask Amelia and she felt she could, now. The trouble was that she didn't know where, how, to begin. She didn't want anyone to know how she felt about Cosmo. After all, she had been told of his attitude towards women, marriage, right from the start. She was a fool to have fallen in love with him, she didn't want to make matters worse by being seen to be a fool.

But for how much longer could she go on like this? Only the other day Amelia had asked whether she would work on the next book, which would go on till the start of November, till Amelia left for Bermuda.

'Is it about the next book?' Amelia probed. 'Is that what's worrying you? Aren't you happy here?'

'Oh, yes! Very. Very. I—it's just . . . may I ask you something, Amelia?'

'Anything.' The old lady looked at her fondly.

'You—you were married once. What happened? I mean, did—did your husband——' She floundered. She was skirting very widely around what she really wanted to know and Amelia must surely think her either nosey or stupid.

Amelia thought no such thing. She simply answered the question. Then she deliberately went on to tell her young friend what she really wanted to know. In any case, it was high time Dawn was told about Cosmo's background. Maybe she would understand him better then.

'He died early on in the war, Dawn. He was home on his first leave when we got married. He was being posted overseas. We had just three days together and then he was sent abroad. And that's where he died, just one month later.'

Three days! Dawn didn't know what to say. *Three days* and then . . . and then her husband never came home. 'Oh, I'm so sorry, Amelia! And in all these years——'

'In all these years, there's never been anyone else. There couldn't have been. Life rarely gives anyone that kind of love twice. John was an extraordinary, special, generous and very loving man. Actually, I hadn't known him all that long, a year or so, before we married . . .' For several seconds Amelia was back in the past, her eyes drifting towards the window as if she could see reflected there the pictures, the memories that were precious to her.

Dawn sat in silence.

'I'd moved in with his parents, they lived about sixty miles from here. They——' Amelia smiled suddenly, her attention going back to Dawn. 'Let me start a little earlier than that. This house belonged to my parents, and when they died they left it to my brother, Gregory, who was Cosmo's father. Gregory was two years older than I; the house and land—and there was more land in those days—was left to him and a fair amount of money was left to me, money which was invested to give me an income. I had never worked, you see, nor was I expected to, or to need to, ever, and by the time our parents died, my brother was already qualified as a doctor, qualified and practising as a general practitioner. But of course he was in the Forces during the war and so we closed Cornerways and I moved in with John's parents.'

'After the war, when Gregory came home, thankfully, we opened the house again and lived here together. He married a girl whom we'd both known all our lives, a Hampshire girl who came from a good family. She was very English, if you know what I mean, her name was Ann and she was a black-haired, black-eyed beauty. She was also a born mother and the most domesticated of creatures.'

Amelia was smiling again, not wistfully this time but with genuine amusement. Seconds later, though still smiling, Dawn saw the light in her eyes fade, to be replaced by an awful, fleeting sadness. 'Of course in those days we had two maids and a housekeeper, a full-time gardener, too, though Ann used to love to help in the garden. That and riding were really the only things that gave her pleasure outside the domain of her home. She loved this house, she loved me, and I loved her very dearly, probably as much as Gregory did, albeit in a different way, of course. We were like sisters. She was an only child and I was to her the sister she never had.

'Ann ran the house, I helped Gregory part-time in his surgery. I taught myself to type and I used to do his letters for him, keep his records and so on. I was to be grateful for that experience later on.

'We all got on so well together, and when Cosmo was born—well, if he wasn't with his mother, he was with me. My role I suppose, was one of spinster aunt, except that I'd been married, I was . . . helper-cum-nanny-cum-companion to Gregory's family.

'Gregory had a very busy practice, he'd be out doing his rounds for hours on end and he was never, ever, too busy to talk to people, or too tired, and very often people called here out of hours, wanting him when he should have been resting. Looking back, I see that he was as much a priest as a doctor. All sorts of people told him their troubles, troubles of a non-medical nature.' She broke off suddenly and her next sentence came out crisply, in an almost business-like manner. 'When Cosmo was six, Ann died of leukaemia. Her illness, her death came astonishingly quickly.'

Amelia waved her small hands impatiently, having no desire to dwell on the details. 'Gregory was mortified. He went inside himself, seemed to turn against that which he had been born to do, practise medicine. He spoke scathingly of "this wonderful progressive science—which couldn't save his own wife". He thought himself useless, impotent . . . of course he was merely mortal.

'As for Cosmo . . . his mother's death and his father's strangeness, albeit a temporary strangeness, affected him deeply. He cried solidly for—I don't care to think about how long. Then Gregory started drinking. In my ignorance of what alcoholism really is, I thought he was turning into an alcoholic. He drank at night and sometimes during the day, but always his mood was black and he had hardly a word to say to anyone on any matter. For a few months we had a locum take over his practice. Everyone understood: the doctor was ill or mourning or temporarily not in his right mind.

'It was only as Gregory recovered that Cosmo recovered. He'd started prep school by then, as a day student, and he began to do well when his father resumed work. Gregory took the boy to school and collected him in the afternoons. They were the best of friends and Gregory spent every spare minute he could with him.

'But *I* knew Gregory wasn't the same man, despite his recovery. When Ann died, something in Gregory died, too, some essential zest for life and for people which had made him so dear not only to me but to everyone who knew him.'

She sighed deeply. This time, there was a long, long pause. Dawn wondered whether that were the end of the story, was just about to speak when Amelia went on: 'For four years life went on uneventfully. From time to time Gregory would go up to London to a conference or a lecture or something. Then, suddenly, he started going up regularly every Saturday and he would come back on Monday morning, in time for his afternoon surgery.'

Amelia's brows went up and she shook her head in an attitude of disbelief. 'One day he came home with a woman on his arm. I remember very clearly their getting out of his car—which was a somewhat battered old Ford. There he was, dressed in his casual tweeds, looking just like a country squire, and there she was clinging to his arm, dressed in furs and looking as though she'd never ridden in anything but Bentleys.

'I remember feeling panic stricken at that instant, though of course I said nothing to Gregory about the woman, on that day or any subsequent day . . .'

'Panic stricken?' The silence had stretched on for so long this time that Dawn simply had to prompt her.

'He was besotted by the woman. Totally, utterly, besotted. I could see that very plainly. He introduced her to me, he showed her the house—and he married her, without warning me, at a Register office in London the following weekend.

'It was *bound* to fail! To this day I can't understand what he was thinking about. Of course, Cosmo was only ten years old, and I for one had hoped Gregory would marry again. But what a choice he made! Gloria was so *wrong* for him, they were so wrong for each other. She was an actress, not a successful one. She was twelve years younger than Gregory and she was extremely beautiful—perhaps too much so for her own good. And she was very much a city girl.'

Amelia shook her head. 'In brief, Dawn, I left this house just four months after they married. Gloria *ordered* me to, but I was leaving anyway. I'd already been looking for somewhere to live and I had found a place.

'Gloria was already three months pregnant and she was utterly miserable. That's something else I don't understand, her getting pregnant. To this day, I don't know whether it was intentional. I *do* know that the girl was bored to death living here—and I know she resented Cosmo awfully.'

As though bracing herself, Amelia took a deep breath and she looked at Dawn uncertainly. An unpleasant, crawling sensation started at the base of Dawn's spine and wriggled its way up as Amelia finished the story. 'I didn't see my brother after I left. I didn't see any of them. The next thing I knew . . . I was told . . . was that Gregory was dead. He'd shot himself after Gloria walked out on him. He got up early one morning, walked about two miles into the woods and shot himself.'

'Oh, God!' Dawn's voice was a whisper. She covered her mouth with her hands, her eyes widened in horror as she absorbed this information and all its implications.

Amelia kept deliberately quiet for a while to give Dawn time to do just that. At length she said, 'I came back here at once, of course. The children were with a friend of Gregory's. Needless to say, Gloria did not take Richie with her when she left. Nobody has seen or heard of her to this day.' She got up, walked slowly round the room. 'Richie was only six weeks old so he was unaffected emotionally, at least at that point. With Cosmo it was a very different story. He was eleven by then and the only thing that had been stable, unchanging, in his short life was *this house*.'

Amelia stabbed a finger in the air in the most forceful, uncharacteristic way, her expression hardening. 'I was determined to keep it and to educate him as Gregory wanted him to be educated. But there was no money.' She turned, staring at nothing. 'There was no money because Gloria had somehow managed to spend it all. Even the land had been sold, acre by acre. I don't—yes I do. I was going to say I don't know how she managed it in such a short time, but I do. Gregory had bought her the furs, the clothes she was wearing the day I met her. He spoiled her terribly, gave her all she wanted—well, all it was in his power to give. He wasn't a rich man, he was comfortable but not rich. Anyhow, it obviously wasn't enough for her.

'So there I was, in my forties, knowing only how to work as a doctor's receptionist, but unable to work because I had two children on my hands, one of whom was a baby. Besides, there were no jobs around here, near this house. And you'll appreciate that my money had dwindled, that what had given me a good income in my parents' day was next to nothing by then. But I was determined to stay here, to keep the family home, for Cosmo far more than for myself . . .'

'And so?'

'And so.' There was an almost impish smile now. 'And so I tried my hand at writing childrens' stories. I tried them out on Cosmo. Besides, I'd always written stories for him, ever since he was old enough to understand them. I was lucky, Dawn. I was published straight away.'

It was Dawn's turn to smile. With affection, with deep admiration, she said, 'No, Amelia. You weren't lucky, you were—are—*talented*. Very talented.'

'Thank you.'

'Thank you,' Dawn said softly. 'Thank you for—for telling me all this. I—I——'

'Yes, it's quite a story, isn't it?' She didn't seem to notice that Dawn felt obliged to say something further. 'Well, dear! I think I'll go down and see how lunch is coming along. I'll see you later . . .'

The library door closed softly and Dawn was left alone with her thoughts. Her mind was boggling with all she'd been told. Amelia had got well and truly carried away and had told her her entire family history. And how glad Dawn was about that! Dear God, it was as though pieces of a jigsaw had all slotted together in her mind, pieces of the picture that was Cosmo, and now she could see the whole. She finally understood him completely.

There was no arguing, no wrestling to be done with herself now. When Cosmo had been eleven years old, at that formative, sensitive age, his father had shot himself for the love of a woman. This, after the boy had witnessed his father's reaction to the death of his wife. The death of Cosmo's mother. What a childhood he'd had!

So this is why he was as he was. Rightly or wrongly, Cosmo was as he was—and nothing on earth would change him or his attitudes.

Dawn accepted that, but it was a long time before she got round to thinking about herself and the love she felt for Cosmo Temple. She wished he had told her this story himself, wished that he would trust her with it, wished fervently he could feel that close to her that he could tell her. He had never, ever, mentioned his parents to Dawn. She hadn't even known that his father was a doctor.

So what should she do now? Having to think about it, having to face the bare reality of the futility of loving Cosmo made her feel sick to her stomach. So she didn't think about it. She couldn't just stop loving him. Nor could she leave him, not when she didn't have to. She would tell Amelia she was prepared to work on the next book ... then she would face November when November came.

What Dawn hadn't accounted for was that in the meantime things got harder for her. There were other facts to face: what did Cosmo do with his evenings in London? With whom did he go out? With whom ... with whom did he make love? She tried desperately, constantly, to push these questions to the back of her mind, reminding herself that he was entitled to do as he wished. He was not committed to her in any way. He was single, he was free—as he would always be. He liked to be himself, without compromise—and he would never compromise. Not for any woman.

He continued to come home at the weekends but

Dawn never fooled herself that he was coming to see her. Of course he enjoyed her company, she knew that much. But he would have enjoyed himself in his beloved home, in his beloved surroundings, just as much if Dawn hadn't been there. There was, after all, his aunt, his surrogate mother, the woman who had held everything together for him when he had desperately needed someone to do that.

She thought about, and dismissed, the idea of having an affair with him just for the remaining months that the paths of their lives would run parallel. That he wanted her at least physically, especially physically, *only* physically, she was well aware. He couldn't have told her more bluntly than he had. But Dawn did not share his attitudes on such matters. To her the act of physical love was something special which should be shared by people who love each other. Perhaps she was an oddity in this day and age. It was not that she didn't love Cosmo enough to give herself to him, it was because she loved him so much that she couldn't, not when he was so calculating, when she knew she would end up as merely a number on the list of women he'd had and had yet to have.

On the third week end in June, Richie came with Cosmo to *Cornerways*. The younger man seemed determined to have a whale of a time and on the Saturday night, he insisted they all went dancing. Amelia was highly amused and she encouraged Dawn and Cosmo to go along with the idea. They did because they understood, as Amelia did, Richie's need for escape. His marriage to Anthea was hanging on a fine thread, and Richie did not want that thread to break. Quite how Anthea felt, Dawn didn't know. Nor did she ask what his wife was doing on the week end Richie made hay.

Made hay? Well, it wasn't quite like that! The disco they ended up in was not as slick, not as swish and thankfully not quite as noisy as the ones Dawn had been to in London. They had all driven nearly as far as Bournemouth to find somewhere which satisfied Richie (they might as well have driven in the other direction, had they known, and gone to London). Needless to say, it was not Cosmo's scene! Nor was it Dawn's, not any longer, she discovered.

She and Cosmo sat uncomfortably on wooden stools in a darkened corner at the furthest point from the loudspeakers. Even so, the flashing lights were dizzying, the music so loud that they had to shout to make themselves heard. Richie had taken off, was dancing energetically with anyone who was willing—and Dawn wasn't aware of it if he got any refusals.

'Look at him!' Cosmo growled at her over the table, shifting on his seat. 'He's like an overgrown kid!'

'He's just letting off steam,' Dawn laughed riotously.

'I know, I know.' Cosmo reached for her hand and held on to it. 'And thanks.'

'What?'

'And thanks,' he shouted, frustrated. 'For putting up with him. Good grief, this place is *awful*. Things weren't like this in my day——'

'What?'

'Forget it! I must be getting old.'

'Getting bold? Why,' she giggled, 'are you going to ask me to dance?'

'I'm—*Yes*!' he yelled. 'As a matter of fact, I am. Anything's better than sitting here on these things.'

'Aw, thank *you*! Such charm! Such finesse! Such tact!'

He roared with laughter. Half an hour later, still dancing, it looked suspiciously to Dawn as though he were actually enjoying himself. And it looked to Cosmo as though she were enjoying herself. But then she was only twenty-three.

'Excuse me!' Dawn was suddenly grabbed from behind by Richie. He had been drinking, but fairly moderately. All one could have accused him of, had one not known what he was going through, was of being overly-merry. 'This *is* an excuse me!'

It was hardly that! The girl who had been dancing with Richie moved vaguely in Cosmo's direction and Richie moved vaguely in Dawn's. It was difficult to tell who was dancing with whom, really, on the tiny, crowded floor.

'I'll have my partner back.' Cosmo yelled at his brother as one noisy record melted into another. 'She looks as though she could use a drink.'

'No, you don't!' Richie caught hold of Dawn's hands, still dancing—and rather well, actually. 'You may take *my* partner for a drink. She deserves it after being seen in public with you. You're not the hottest thing on two feet, you know!'

Cosmo and Dawn exchanged looks while the other poor girl looked on. He gave a swift look heavenward, she gave a swift nod. Cosmo duly took the purple-haired girl off in the direction of the bar and when they were out of earshot, Dawn laughed until her sides ached.

They had been gone about five minutes when the music changed to something which was more to Dawn's liking. It was a slow number and she looked round automatically, scanning the Saturday night crowd for Cosmo. She couldn't see him. In any case Richie caught hold of her by the waist and pulled her into his arms. 'Won't I do for this one?' He was laughing at her, reading her mind. 'I'm far better looking than he is and besides, he's a bit old for you, probably red-hot on the slow foxtrot, but not this sort of thing . . .'

He pulled her ridiculously close but Dawn went along with it, understanding, knowing it was harmless. There was the strong smell of whisky on his breath as he chattered to her but she didn't let that worry her, either. She felt sorry for him, that's all. Besides, he was Cosmo's brother . . .

'It's not often I can steal a girl from Cosmo,' he rambled, his mouth close to her ear. 'In fact, I've only done it once before, and I married her.'

'Really?' Dawn pulled away slightly in order to look at him, unsure whether he were serious.

He pulled her back. 'Really.' She was in fact only half listening as he went on to say how beautiful Anthea was, how she could have got any man she set her sights on. Instead she was thinking how slight his body felt compared to Cosmo's. It was only when he added, 'Except Cosmo' that Dawn gave him her full attention.

'What do you mean?'

'I mean I stole Anthea from Cosmo. But she wouldn't have got him in any case, as I'm sure you realise. He's not the marrying kind. But she wanted him, I know it.'

Dawn was really confused now. She was also alarmed. 'So you were serious a minute ago—when you said you'd, I mean, am I to understand that Cosmo was going out with Anthea before she married you?'

'Yep. Why, what of it? What's the big deal?'

'Well, it—it happens, I suppose. No, there's no big deal. It's just . . .' She couldn't say it, couldn't bring herself to ask whether Cosmo and Richie's wife had been lovers . . .

'It's just that you want to know whether he laid her.' Richie said it for her—only far more bluntly than she would have put it.

'Richie, I didn't——'

'That's what you were wondering, pretty lady.' He was laughing at her, unperturbed. 'The answer is that I don't know. He hadn't been seeing her for long. When he introduced me to her, I fell head over heels in love with her on sight. Bang! That was it. And I'm still in love with the bitch.'

'Richie——' It was getting too much. Dawn didn't want to hear any more. She was disturbed by this conversation and she didn't like the raw bitterness she'd heard when Richie came out with his last sentence. Still, she could hardly clamp a hand over his mouth, could hardly close her ears when he went on.

'Cosmo saw what happened to me. Well, I told him, anyway. And he warned me off her right from the start. But of course that didn't make me fall out of love.' He laughed, there was no bitterness now, just a sort of resignation. 'My own opinion was that Cosmo had never made love to her, but I didn't want to ask because I knew he'd tell me the truth and I didn't want to know if he had. However, in retrospect, having subsequently learned that my darling wife is something of a nymphomaniac, I shouldn't be surprised to——'

'Richie, please! I *don't* want to hear this.'

'But, Dawn, what does it matter now? I honestly don't care——'

He never got to finish his sentence. Cosmo appeared right behind him and goodnaturedly disengaged him from Dawn. 'That's quite enough of that, young man. Hands *off*.' He was laughing but it seemed to Dawn there was a good deal of seriousness behind the words. Richie let go of Dawn at once, stepping back. Fifty minutes later, still laughing and jovial, they headed for home.

But Dawn's laughter had been a little forced towards

the end; she'd had to make an effort. Going home in
the car, she was quiet, quiet and tired. It had been
tremendous fun, the entire evening—until that conversation with Richie. It bothered her enormously. Had
Cosmo and Anthea been lovers? He hadn't been seeing
the woman for long, Richie said, and Richie should
know, but still . . . had they? Of course it didn't matter
to Dawn, but how could Richie not mind? He didn't,
she was convinced of it, was sure that any such
resentment would show through. But there was no
resentment, his relationship with Cosmo was a good
one, his respect for his older brother was clear for
anyone to see.

'How about a nightcap?' The suggestion came from
Richie when they trooped indoors as quietly as possible,
like thieves in the night. It was almost three in the
morning.

Cosmo did not tell him he'd had enough, which he
had, instead he was more cunning. 'How about making
yourself scarce while I say good night to Dawn?'

Richie actually apologised! 'Oh! Of course. Sorry!'
Without further ado, he made himself scarce and
Cosmo flinched as they heard him stumble up the stairs.

Dawn flopped tiredly into a chair, not too tiredly that
she couldn't spare the energy to glare at Cosmo. 'You
realise you've now given him quite the wrong
impression about us?'

'I realise. Dammit.' He flopped down, too. He didn't
even bother with a drink.

'Is that an apology?'

'No, it's a lament that the impression I gave him isn't
an accurate one!'

'You're incorrigible, Cosmo!' She tried to laugh.

He looked at her. 'And you,' he said seriously, 'are
upset about something. For heaven's sake, the idiot

didn't make a pass at you on the dance floor, did he? If he did, I hope you realise——'

'No, no, of *course* not. Of course he didn't!'

'Then what's worrying you?'

'Nothing.' She couldn't talk about it, didn't want to.

'Dawn——' There was a warning note in his voice but she didn't respond 'Come on,' he said then, reasonably, 'out with it. You once harboured a grudge against me in the past and it was all based on a misunderstanding, remember?'

She remembered. Still she said nothing.

'Please, Dawn. I know you, I can read you, what's wrong? Don't have me half out of my mind all night—*tell* me.'

Because he coaxed her, she told him. Because she was so idiotically pleased that he might worry over her being upset, she told him. 'It—Richie told me that you'd been taking Anthea out before he met her, is that right?'

'Yes.' The word came on an upswing, as though he were intrigued.

'He—oh, dear, this is awful, Cosmo. He called her names even while he said he was in love with her still. He said—said she's something of a nymphomaniac.'

He considered that, taking it very seriously. 'I'd say that's something of an exaggeration.' He still didn't know where this was leading, why Dawn should be perturbed. 'Ah!' When he realised what was going through her mind, he smiled. 'And you want to know whether I ever made love to Anthea.'

'No! No, I don't! It's just—just that I can't understand why Richie never asked you. It's—I would have had to, had I been in a similar position.'

'Which is purely hypothetical.' He smiled but he did not seem happy with the conversation. 'Richie never asked me the question.'

'He said he didn't want to because you would have given him an honest answer and he said he didn't want to know if you had . . .'

'And so I would.' She saw his jaw tighten. 'And now, Dawn, are you about to ask the question?'

'No.' She didn't want to know, either, but for very different reasons. Whether Richie would have minded or not, it all seemed . . . not right . . . to Dawn.

'I'm very glad to hear it.' Cosmo accepted what she'd said but he was searching her eyes. 'Now listen, Richie didn't ask me whether I'd ever made love to Anthea, but on the eve of his wedding I told him that there had never been anything between me and the girl he was about to marry. I knew he must have wondered about it, to say the least, so I made a point of telling him.'

Dawn nodded, relieved. Richie hadn't mentioned *this*. She got to her feet, kicked off her high-heeled sandals and picked them up.

'Just a minute.' Cosmo was watching her minutely. 'I have a question for you.'

'Yes?'

'Do you believe what I've just told you?'

'Of course I do.' And so she did. And, oh, she was tired. All she wanted now was to fall into bed and sleep till nature woke her. Thank goodness it was Sunday tomorrow!

'Just a minute——' The tone of his voice halted her as she reached the door. 'That was only half the question. What I really want to know is—why should you care? About this business, about the past?'

'I—don't really know. I——' She stopped dead. She wasn't being truthful, and that was wrong of her. He had been entirely truthful with her. 'All right. To tell you the truth, I would have found the idea of your having made love to your brother's wife somewhat distasteful, even though you knew her first, even though you wouldn't have dreamed that Richie would fall in love with her and marry her. Now aren't I a dear old-fashioned thing?' She was mocking herself now but Cosmo did not join in that mockery, did not take, for once, the opportunity of teasing her on her ideas, her morals.

Rather he seemed very distracted suddenly. He looked down at the carpet, a muscle working in his jaw. 'Very,' he said. Then he looked at her directly. 'And don't knock it, it's part of your charm. Goodnight, Dawn.'

Exhausted, she got into bed and for once she didn't even clean her teeth before doing so. It was, she thought, almost a luxury not to have to do that. Was she tipsy? She had had several drinks, true enough, though not as many as Richie had. Cosmo was the only one who'd stayed strictly sober because he'd been driving.

But she couldn't sleep. Nor could she understand why she couldn't sleep. She came to the conclusion that she was just too tired to sleep. Her body was exhausted but her mind ... her mind was going round in circles and she couldn't seem to stop it.

If she had known then that she would meet the mysterious Anthea in the morning, curiosity might have kept her awake all night. As it was, she eventually wound down sufficiently to fall into a deep, deep sleep.

CHAPTER TEN

DAWN woke with a start, as if from a nightmare. But there had been no nightmare, she hadn't even dreamed, as far as she remembered. The sun was streaming through the beige curtains at her window, she could hear the birds singing, and with a groan she thumped her pillow and tried to go back to sleep. Glancing at her clock she was convinced it was only just daybreak—or at the latest eight o'clock.

The clock told her it was eleven.

She couldn't believe it. She sat bolt upright and thought immediately of Amelia, who would be working in the library. It was seconds before she remembered it was Sunday, that at this hour Amelia and Mrs Watt would have gone to Church. It really didn't matter if she stayed in bed till tea time. Of course she didn't. Cosmo was here. She got up at once and walked rather dazedly into her bathroom. Dear Lord, she must have had too much to drink the night before! It was all just very slightly hazy—the memory of last night. It had been fun, it had been disturbing, but it had all ended up very satisfactorily and even though she was not at her brightest, she was happy. Cosmo was here.

After a long, luxurious bath she slipped into a white dress which was made from cheesecloth, nothing fancy but appropriate for a summery Sunday. On her way downstairs she heard the slam of a car door, assuming it was Mrs Watt and Amelia coming back from Church. That was what she assumed; she had lost track of the time by then.

It was only as she approached the drawing room door that she realised her mistake. The door had not been closed properly by the person who had just walked in there; it was ajar, and Dawn realised that it had not been Mrs Watt's Mini which had stopped outside the house only when she heard Cosmo's voice saying angrily, 'Anthea! What the hell are you doing here?' Then, wearily, vaguely apologetically, 'Look, I did ask you not to come here. I asked you not to come *here*.'

Dawn should have walked into the room then. She should have, but something prevented her from doing so. As it was, she found herself standing perfectly still outside the door, hardly daring to move in case she was heard and was thought to be eavesdropping. Yet she was eavesdropping, she realised worriedly. She didn't know what to do as the conversation went on, clearly audible, didn't know whether to go in or whether to backtrack upstairs . . .

'Yes, darling, but I came to see my husband.' Anthea's voice was soft, a mixture of sarcasm and amusement. 'Any objection?'

There was no answer, just a brief silence. 'Where is he?'

'He's still in bed.'

'Drunk again?'

There was another silence. Dawn held her breath.

'Maybe I'll go upstairs and wake him,' Anthea laughed. It was soft, mischievous laughter, and Dawn found herself fraught with curiosity. She wanted to see what this woman looked like in the flesh. She was also frantic because she would be caught red-handed if Anthea walked out of the drawing room.

'Leave him alone, Anthea. Do me a favour and get out of this house before Amelia gets back.'

'Cosmo! How unkind. Amelia will be delighted to see me.'

'Amelia will be disturbed.'

'You're the one who's disturbed by my presence, Cosmo.' There was the tinkle of laughter, the rustle of a newspaper.

'Knock it off, Anthea. It's over. Face it.'

'I'd appreciate a cup of coffee . . .'

'You know where the kitchen is.' Cosmo sounded bored, uninterested, and Dawn's heart leapt into her throat. She moved quickly, stealthily towards the stairs and started to climb them silently, but not before she heard Anthea's next remark: 'Can I make you a cup? Black, without sugar, if I remember correctly.'

She wouldn't have heard Cosmo's answer if it hadn't come out so angrily. 'Get your coffee and then get out of here! You're knocking on a closed door!'

'I . . .'

But that was as much as Dawn caught. She went back upstairs and stood on the landing, unable to make sense of what she'd heard. Why on earth had Anthea come here? Surely she couldn't be missing Richie— unfortunately. Or was she? Why had Cosmo told her so bluntly that she was knocking on a closed door, that it was over? Wouldn't he want to help to save his brother's marriage, if he could?

One thing was certain as far as Dawn was concerned: she couldn't stand on the landing all day! With a somewhat artificial cough followed by a vague, forced hum, she sauntered down the stairs in such a way that no one could be unaware of her presence.

She went straight into the kitchen, as she would have done on any normal day, and said a surprised, polite hello when she saw a stranger filling the kettle at the sink.

Anthea turned, her eyes sweeping over Dawn from head to foot.

Dawn smiled. 'You must be Anthea. I recognise you from your wedding photo.' The older woman was more beautiful than she appeared in the photograph. She had about her a certain quality which is hard to define, a sort of sultry look about her features which, combined with a sparkling vivacity, made one want to study her face in minute detail. She was, simply, stunning. She had been a photographic model and the style, the flair her profession demanded was evident in her extremely subtle make-up, her poise, her clothes. Even standing at the sink, kettle in hand, she managed to look like someone from the pages of a magazine. Her black, silky hair was gathered almost demurely into an intricate knot at her nape, she was considerably taller than Dawn and perfectly proportioned.

Very green, almond-shaped eyes were looking at Dawn with equal interest. 'And you're the little Welsh girl I've heard so much about. I've wondered about you, Dawn, and now that I've seen you, I need wonder no more.'

This was said nicely, casually, but it made Dawn's eyebrows go up. 'I'm not sure what you mean. Here, let me do that.'

Anthea willingly let her make the coffee, was content to stand back, arms folded, and continue her surveillance while Dawn busied herself with cups and saucers and things. 'I mean that I can now understand what the attraction is down here—apart from the scenery, of course.'

Uneasy, Dawn turned to look at her. What on *earth* was she implying? 'I—look, your husband coming here has nothing to do with me, I can assure you. All he was in need of this weekend was some relaxation.'

'There's no need to get uptight, dear. It wasn't my husband I was referring to. I've been curious to see what it is that brings Cosmo back to Cornerways every weekend.'

'This is his home,' Dawn said briskly, 'as I'm sure you're aware.' She was annoyed. Why should it matter to Anthea if Cosmo came home every weekend? And she didn't care for being given the once-over like this, either.

'I'm sorry.' Anthea spoke with what sounded like sincerity. 'Please don't take offence. It's just that Cosmo never used to come here every weekend, not *every* weekend, religiously. Or perhaps you don't realise how extraordinary you are? There are very few women who can hold his attention for long—surely you know that? Or maybe nobody's told you.'

'I've been told.'

'Good for you.' There was a friendly smile now, a girl-to-girl wink as Anthea put what she thought was an end to the conversation. 'So you'll just enjoy it while it lasts, eh? Quite right, too—my sentiments entirely! But whatever you do, don't fall in love with the man.' She turned to walk out of the kitchen.

'Just a minute!' Dawn plonked down the tray she'd just picked up so hard that everything on it rattled. She was seeing red. '*I'm* not the one who's having an affair with someone, *Mrs Temple*. Not that this is any of your business. I think you——' She broke off sharply as the kitchen door opened, closing her eyes in dread that she'd been overheard by Amelia or the housekeeper. Richie's aunt was aware that his marriage was not a happy one—but she didn't know the half of it. Both Cosmo and Richie protected her from the truth.

'Anthea!' It was Richie. Dawn sagged with relief, seeing the look of pleasure on his face as his eyes alighted on his wife. It was fleeting, replaced quickly by something approaching resentment. 'Why have you come here?'

Anthea was looking at Dawn as she responded, not answering his question. 'My, my Richie, you have painted a very black picture of me to your little Welsh friend. She seems to think I'm having an affair with someone.'

'Come off it, Anthea. You've been having an affair with someone for the past six months. And this isn't the first. You don't know what the word faithful means.'

The older woman merely smiled. She reached out to touch her husband's cheek, and he let her, closing his eyes as if her touch gave him pain. 'You're mistaken, Richie. I've told you and told you. Would I be here now if I were having an affair with someone? Wouldn't I have taken this opportunity, while you were away for the weekend, to see my lover?'

Dawn stood there, mesmerised, watching as Richie spoke through clenched teeth. But he still didn't brush her hand away. 'No, darling, you wouldn't. Your lover is married, that much I have worked out. You never see him at weekends.'

'Quite the little detective, aren't you? Evidence Richie? Have you got any? No! Because you're imagining all this and I'm——'

'Okay, that's enough!' Cosmo's voice startled all of them. His face was taut with anger. 'Mrs Watt and Amelia have just pulled up. Now come into the drawing room, all of you, and cut out the bickering.'

They both responded, Richie and Anthea, and Dawn turned to pick up the tray. Unsure whether she was included in Cosmo's anger, she was relieved when he took the tray from her and flashed her a smile.

'Anthea! How lovely to see you! It's been too long, dear.' Amelia's presence brought normality to the scene, though it didn't manage to clear the atmosphere, not quite. All the younger people were tense, in varying degrees.

'Now what are your plans?' Amelia went on, 'Are you staying for the day? You'll drive back with Richie later, I suppose?'

'Yes, I—well, we'll be in separate cars, but yes.'

'Good! That means you're staying for lunch. That's all I wanted to know. I'll just go and tell Mrs Watt.'

'I'll do it.' Cosmo got to his feet, shaking his head slightly as he walked past Dawn. She knew what he was thinking: he'd wanted to get rid of Anthea and now it was too late.

Major Wright came over for lunch and in the middle of the afternoon, the Vicar called. Around four-thirty, Cosmo signalled Dawn with his eyes—'Do you want to escape for a while?'

Her blue eyes signalled in the affirmative and she and Cosmo extracted themselves, without causing any offence to anyone, saying they were going for a walk.

In fact they went for a drive. They drove in comfortable, tension-free silence for half an hour, until Cosmo drew the Jensen to a halt. 'That was some afternoon, mm? Come on, let's walk to the lakeside.'

They were both glad to be away from the house, both glad to be alone together. They walked, hand in hand, Dawn stooping occasionally to pick up a daisy or a buttercup. 'Is it safe to leave those two with Amelia?' she asked at length.

'Yes. Especially with old Eustace Wright and the Vicar present!' He looked down at her, smiling. 'You're looking very pretty today, Miss. Shall we sit down?'

'And spoil my dress?' She was joking, the grass was perfectly dry, the sun was shining and it was a glorious day—now.

'You can sit on my legs.'

'I'll sit on the grass, thank you!'

He caught hold of her wrists, pulling her towards him

as his grey-black eyes looked laughingly into hers. 'Still don't trust me, eh?' He didn't give her time to answer. He stooped and planted a swift, chaste kiss on her lips. 'There, now how's that for self-control?'

'Admirable!'

Then, much to her chagrin, he plucked from her hand one of the daisies she'd collected, pulled a petal from it and said, 'She loves me, she loves me not . . .'

Foolishly she wanted to cry. She wanted to put her arms around him, lean her head on his chest and say, she loves you. She loves you, Cosmo, she has done for a long time. Instead she looked up at him, managing a giggle. 'Well? What's the verdict?'

He threw away what was left of the flower, caught her chin in his hands. 'Why don't I see for myself?'

He looked directly into her eyes, eyes which were doing their utmost to keep all emotion out of them, to reflect nothing but a mild amusement. 'Wishy-washy,' he pronounced, grinning. 'That's what your feelings for me are.' He picked another flower. 'Your turn.'

'I don't need a daisy to tell me how you feel about me, Cosmo!' She managed, she managed nicely to laugh it off—all of it. 'It's obvious!'

But he wasn't laughing. 'Is it?' he asked quietly. And then he was kissing her, without passion. The flowers fell from her fingers and they stood for a long time with their arms around one another, their mouths meeting and separating, meeting and separating, merely enjoying the warmth, the taste of one another, the comfort of the bodily contact.

Gently he put an arm around her shoulder and they sat on the grass by the side of the lake. 'How's the book coming along?'

'It's finished. Well, Amelia's finished writing. I have a couple more days' work to do. Two or three . . .

anyhow, we've planned to take it in to the publishers next Friday. We thought we'd use it as an excuse to go shopping in London for the day! Maybe we can all meet for lunch? You and Richie?'

'Richie will be in New York by then, he'll be away for a couple of weeks. But you'll see me, come to my flat around noon, then that'll give you plenty of time to shop afterwards. And come up by train, I'll drive us back here in the evening.'

'Lovely! Actually, I'm half-wishing Amelia wasn't coming with me. I could have taken the opportunity of shopping for a dress for the party next month.' The birthday party was in fact only two weeks away, two weeks today, on the Sunday, and Dawn had yet to buy a gift for Amelia, too. 'As it is, if I buy something swish to wear, she's bound to ask me what it's for! Which reminds me, how are we going to get her to London, me, Mrs Watt and all, without her guessing something?'

Cosmo had already anticipated that. 'Simple. I'm going to tell her I'm taking her out for a very special dinner—which will solve your shopping problem next Friday. I'll say it's a family affair—which of course includes Mrs Watt. She's almost one of the family. I'll mention it before I leave tonight.'

Laughing, excited about the whole thing, Dawn said, 'And me? What am I?'

He just looked at her. 'I'll tell you what it feels like, it feels as though you're one of the family.'

It was meant as a compliment, she supposed, but it was a very far cry from how she wanted him to feel about her. 'How boring, Cosmo!' She looked at him impishly, teasing him as she lay back on the grass. 'I didn't realise your feelings towards me were *brotherly*!'

'*Brotherly!* Who said——' All laughter faded suddenly, for her, for him, as he lay down beside her and gathered her into his arms. He didn't kiss her, he held her very close, his mouth just inches from hers. 'Dawn, don't you know how much I want you? All I'm waiting for is for you to . . .'

She put a finger over his lips. He was about to spoil this beautiful time together. She didn't want to hear it, didn't want to be reminded that he was waiting for her agreement to have an affair with him. 'Don't, Cosmo.' She could feel the prickle of tears at the back of her eyes and she prayed they would not become visible to him. 'You're about to spoil things again. I thought we had an understanding? I thought I'd made it clear that I don't want an affair with you?'

There was silence for a moment. 'Yet you want me. You want me but you don't want me.'

'That's right. That's precisely how it is.'

He sighed, still holding her, his eyes still searching hers. A strange calm had come over her. He knew full well the power he had to arouse her—but she knew he wouldn't use it. He wanted her compliance, more than merely the compliance of her body. Gratefully she realised she was not in any danger of crying now. 'You know, Dawn, you are one woman I don't understand very well.'

She didn't know how to answer that without letting him know more than she wanted him to know. She looked beyond him to a bird which was rustling the leaves of a tree a few yards away.

Very slightly, Cosmo's arms tightened around her, his voice barely audible as he spoke. 'Dear God, you are beautiful, Dawn . . .'

No. She wasn't. Pretty, yes, but she wasn't beautiful. She just smiled, her eyes moving slowly up to look at the sky, blue looking at blue. And then there was his voice again, soft, gentle, his lips brushing ever so lightly against her ear. 'And if I told you that I love you, Dawn, would that make any difference?'

It was more than enough to make her lose her composure, more than enough to bring back those threatening tears. In that instant she almost hated him. Dear God, that he would resort to this! She would never have believed it of him.

She pulled away from him, getting quickly to her feet. 'You disappoint me, Cosmo.' Quickly she turned her back on him for fear he would see that her eyes were unnaturally bright. In a voice which she hoped sounded careless, cool, she added, 'It would make no difference at all.'

CHAPTER ELEVEN

'BUT it doesn't matter at all, Amelia. We can post the manuscript—or we can take it in on Monday. We'll see how you feel then.' Dawn was sitting on Amelia's bed. She had got up early, looking forward to their day in London—and had been told by Mrs Watt that Amelia was feeling unwell, that she had a slight temperature.

'It does matter. You've been looking forward to a trip round the shops. I want you to go, Dawn. Heavens, you don't need me to go with you! You're not likely to get lost!'

'I'm going to stay right here and look after you.'

'You'll do no such thing! I've got Mrs Watt to do that. Besides, Cosmo's expecting you——'

'He's expecting *us*.'

'I'll come up next week.' Amelia was firm. 'Do your shopping today, then next week we'll go up together and you can help me choose something for this dinner he's giving me for my birthday. All right?'

'We-ell . . .'

'I'll be fine, don't worry. And I'll ring Cosmo shortly to explain what's happening. Now off you *go*!'

Cosmo. She thought about him during her train journey to London. When wasn't she thinking about him? She watched the scenery from the windows of the train without really seeing anything. Last Sunday, hours after Richie and Anthea had left, Cosmo had taken leave of his home with the reluctance he always showed when doing so. He had kissed her and his aunt briefly on the cheek and had left Cornerways around nine in the evening.

But Dawn's overriding memory of him, of last weekend, was when he had said, quite simply, 'I see.' This, after she had told him it would make no difference to her at all, his saying he loved her. She hadn't been looking at him, she had stood with her back to him, afraid he would see her tears. She had never expected him to resort to lies in order to coax her into his bed. Not for one minute dared she think that there might, just might, have been some truth in his words. She was not prone to self-deception, she never had been.

London was throbbing with life and she couldn't help feeling excited at being in the city again. For a visit, it was super. There was no time for her to get any shopping in before lunch, however. By the time she'd extracted herself from the publisher, who'd chatted over coffee about the book and her work on it, Dawn had to hop into a taxi and head for Cosmo's flat. She was expected there at noon.

She was admitted by a tall, immaculate, poker-faced man whose name, he said, was Thomas. 'Do come in, Miss Davies. Mr Temple has just telephoned. He asked me to give you his apologies; he'll be half an hour late leaving his office.'

He led Dawn into the living room and her eyes widened in surprise. This place was nothing at all like Cornerways!

Thomas offered her a drink. She asked for a sherry and told him she was going to take a look round. He showed her the kitchen, from which delicious smells were emanating, then left her to wander. Thomas was cooking lunch, and by the look of things it was going to be something special.

Cosmo's second home was hardly a flat. It was a four-bedroomed apartment complete with dining room, study, a large living room opening on to a balcony which overlooked Hyde Park. It must have cost him a fortune! It was light, airy, spacious, the luxury of the carpets and furnishings almost decadent! It was only when she put her head round the door of Cosmo's bedroom that she realised she should perhaps not be doing this. He might have wanted to show her round himself—maybe she was being a bit presumptuous? No, Thomas had made no objection, had seemed to take it for granted even. Cosmo's manservant had obviously been told who Dawn was.

Cosmo's bedroom was predominantly burgundy and white, the furnishings modern but expensive. The sun was streaming through windows which were curtained with burgundy velvet and the same material covered the king-size bed which dominated the room. Dawn didn't linger in there; she poked her head into the adjoining bathroom and then retreated. As she stepped back into the bedroom something caught her eye, something glistening. She turned, trying to identify what it was, where it was. As she turned her head again, it happened again and she glanced at the mirror on the wardrobe door, on which the sun was shining. Something absolutely brilliant was being reflected and she couldn't see what . . .

And then she spotted it.

It was an ear-ring. It was nestling on the floor by the leg of the dressing-table and had it not been for the sunlight, it would have been virtually invisible against the whiteness of the carpet. With a sinking heart, Dawn picked it up. It was of the clip-on type, a tiny pearl surrounded by chips of diamond. It was also the real thing, exquisite.

For long seconds she stood, looking at the jewels in her hand, feeling jealous of its owner and resentment for the man whose bedroom this was. She gave herself a mental shake, biting her lip. Why was she so shocked, so disappointed? Had she thought that Cosmo had changed his life-style since meeting her? Had she thought he lived like a monk? No. No, she hadn't thought that.

She had refused to dwell on thoughts about his life in London.

So much for his saying he loved her!

She put the ear-ring back exactly where she had found it. It would probably end up in Cosmo's vacuum cleaner.

Too bad!

'Sorry I'm late.' Cosmo greeted her with a swift kiss some twenty minutes later. 'I hope Thomas looked after you all right?'

'Yes.' She watched him as he sank tiredly on to one of the two settees in the living room, loosening his tie. 'I—had a look round, I hope you don't mind?'

He smiled. 'My home is your home, you should know that. You're as welcome here as you are at Cornerways, my lovely.'

'I must say this place is very different from Cornerways.'

'Ah, well, as far as I'm concerned, that's Amelia's house. I mean,' he grinned, 'it's kept in a state of preservation, if you like. In it, she preserves the past. She was brought up there, you know.'

'Yes, she—told me that.' Dawn glanced around, still making an effort to conceal the shock she'd had just twenty minutes earlier. The shock which should not have been a shock. 'You have a lot of rooms here, Cosmo. Did Richie live here with you before he got married?'

'Good grief, no. He had a flat in Hampstead. Now he

has a house—*they've* got a house in Wimbledon, not far from Jeremy Wright, actually. He has a house in that area. Which reminds me, have you seen anything of him lately?'

Dawn had seen Jeremy only once since her somewhat unusual evening out with him. 'About three weeks ago. He was visiting his father for the day and they both came to lunch. He'll be at the party, I suppose? Jeremy, I mean?' She knew, of course, that the Major would be there.

'Oh, yes. Probably with some outrageously extrovert actress on his arm. Anyhow, what's all this about Amelia? She 'phoned me this morning to say that you were coming, but she wasn't. Said she was feeling off-colour. What does that mean, exactly?'

'Just that. I don't think there's any call for worry. You'll see for yourself tonight.'

They went their separate ways after lunch—a splendid lunch. Dawn headed for the shops and Cosmo went back to his office, where she was to meet him at six o'clock. For her, however, the excitement had gone from the day. Even the thought of the weekend ahead with Cosmo couldn't put it back.

She strolled from shop to shop distractedly, unable to concentrate on what she was looking for. To whom did that ear-ring belong? How long had Cosmo been seeing the woman . . . *sleeping* with her?

Throughout lunch, though she had talked with him as easily and naturally as she always did, Dawn had wanted to accuse him. She had wanted to tell him what she'd found in his bedroom and demand to know all about the woman. But of course she couldn't, wouldn't. She had no right to do that. He and she were merely friends without any form of commitment between them.

Her shopping trip was unsuccessful, she actually

ended up empty-handed, having bought nothing at all. Cosmo teased her about that as they drove down to the New Forest—to a weekend which turned out to be a complete flop.

Amelia had what turned out to be a summer cold, the worst kind, and she spent the weekend in bed. Cosmo was tired and disinclined to go riding, walking, anything. Aware that he was deliberately delegating to his brother as much work as possible these days, including the New York trip Richie was now on, Dawn couldn't help wondering about the probable reason for his tiredness. Maybe, like her, he was simply ready for a holiday. But it was far more likely that he'd been having too many late nights for too long. . .

Her own mood, she had to admit, did not help the weekend to go well.

By the following Tuesday, Amelia was up and about. On Wednesday she told Dawn they would go to London on the Friday, that she would feel up to it by then.

On Thursday, Amelia apologetically changed her mind.

Dawn was stretched out on a sun-lounger, revelling in the brilliant sunshine, clad in a bikini. She had skipped lunch because it was just too hot to eat today, but Amelia had gone to the Major's for lunch. She got back around three o'clock and it was then that she changed the plans for the following day.

'Dawn, dear, you won't mind if I don't go to London with you tomorrow, will you?'

Dawn sat up, alarmed. The party was this coming Sunday and she hoped desperately that Amelia wasn't having some sort of relapse. 'Oh, Amelia! Are you ill? What's wrong? I thought it was just a cold and——'

'No, no!' Amelia's small hands were fluttering. 'It

was just a cold. I'm perfectly well. How could I not be in weather like this?' She turned her face up to the sun, closing her eyes as she smiled, seeming amused about something.

'Then what is it? Why aren't you coming to London?'

'Eustace has asked me to spend a couple of days away with him. Just for the weekend. I accepted because ... well, as a matter of fact I want to spend some time with him, in private.'

'Oh!' Dawn didn't know what else to say. Then, horrified, 'But you *can't*! I mean, I mean Sunday—I mean, your birthday! Cosmo—Cosmo will have booked somewhere nice and he'd be——'

'He'd be hurt if I didn't show up.' Amelia was frowning and laughing at the same time. 'Good gracious, I know that! Eustace and I will be there, not to worry.' She leaned over and patted Dawn's hand, calming her, amused at her over-reaction—and a little puzzled by it. 'Now listen, it's all arranged. I just 'phoned Cosmo while I was at Eustace's, and everything's sorted out ...'

She took a big breath, seeming very pleased with herself as she told Dawn what was what. 'Eustace is coming for me first thing in the morning. We're going to spend a couple of days in Bath, at a nice little hotel he knows there. We'll drive to London on Sunday, in time for lunch at Cosmo's.

'Mrs Watt will go up by train on Sunday morning and she'll be there in time for lunch, too. You, my dear, will go tomorrow morning, as planned, and spend the weekend with Cosmo.'

'But—who organised the last bit?'

'Well, I suppose that was Cosmo's idea but it makes sense, doesn't it? Why, is something wrong?'

'No! I—it's just——' It was just that she was taken

aback. It was just that it would feel different, somehow, spending the weekend in London with Cosmo. It wasn't quite the same thing as spending time here with him; here, where there was always Amelia and Mrs Watt . . .

'Dawn?'

She couldn't tell the old lady what was going through her mind, couldn't say that she didn't want to be alone with her nephew. It might sound silly, or shocking, or— something. Amelia had no idea how Dawn felt about Cosmo. 'Yes, it does make sense, of course. I was—just thinking about the shopping. You were going to buy something new for—for your birthday.'

Amelia really was in a happy mood today. She was laughing again. 'My dear, don't be deceived by the fact that you've seen me mainly in slacks and blouses. I have half a wardrobe full of things I've bought in the past and never worn—never had *occasion* to wear. I shall dig something out—and don't worry, I won't let you down.'

There was, it seemed, no more to be said on the matter.

Dawn flopped on to the settee in a state of utter exhaustion. The poker-faced Thomas brought her a tray of tea and biscuits and she looked at him gratefully. Cosmo hadn't got in from work yet; Dawn had spent the day shopping, her feet were throbbing and she was extremely grateful to be in the cool, air-conditioned atmosphere of Cosmo's flat.

'Thank you, Thomas. I have never been so desperate for a cup of tea!'

He gave her a slight bow. She had left with him that morning the small suitcase she'd brought with her and had gone off immediately in the direction of Knightsbridge. 'I unpacked for you this morning, Miss.

Mr Temple had told me you'd be sleeping in the blue guest room. May I take those in for you?'

He was nodding in the direction of the assorted shopping bags Dawn had come in with. 'Yes, please.'

He actually allowed himself a small smile. 'I hope it was worth it? It is rather hot for shopping . . .'

It had been worth it, though. Dawn had found just the right dress—at the last minute. If necessary, she could have resumed her hunt on Saturday, but she didn't want to. Today had been quite enough; tomorrow, she wanted to relax. She was going to stay *right here* in this blissful air-conditioning!

Cosmo had different ideas about that.

Over dinner that evening, he protested. Strongly. 'What do you mean, you're not setting foot outside the door?' He refilled her wine glass, scowling at her. Thomas had produced another superb meal, but Dawn had been warned that Saturday was his day off and that if she wanted breakfast, she'd have to make it herself.

'I mean I'm staying right here, where it's cool.'

'I thought we'd go out for the day, out of London. I thought it would be nice to . . . no? But you don't even know what I was going to suggest! Some company you are!'

'You,' she said, 'can do as you wish. I've told you what I'm going to do. Besides, you spent last weekend stretched out on the settee! So I'm entitled!'

'I was tired, not afraid of the heat.'

Dawn looked down at the white linen tablecloth, all her resentment suddenly resurfacing, not that she had been able to swallow it completely; she was merely trying to live with it. But it wasn't easy. The ear-ring in his bedroom—and his tiredness last weekend.

'Dawn? What is it?'

She shook her head and put a smile on her face. 'Nothing.'

'There's something on your mind. You haven't been yourself—not quite yourself—all evening. So tell me.' He reached for her hand and she had to steel herself not to pull away.

'I'm just tired.' He had once told her that her eyes reflected her emotions and so, now, she made a conscious effort not to let that happen. She looked directly at him. 'That's all.'

But he wasn't fooled. He jumped to his own conclusions and a second later he was grinning. 'It's being here, isn't it? You're on edge because we're not chaperoned.'

Thomas didn't count, of course. He lived in, but his rooms were beyond the kitchen, somewhat separated from the rest of the apartment. Besides, he was no doubt aware of all his master's activities. His employer was, after all, a bachelor.

'Yes.' She said that because his assumption was partly the reason for her distraction. She was certainly on guard.

'Still don't trust me then? You're waiting for me to pounce?' He was laughing at her, she could see it in his eyes. 'Or maybe it's yourself you don't trust?'

He was wrong there. Dawn was in no danger of getting carried away when in the forefront of her mind was the knowledge that he spent his week-days sleeping with others. Or at least one woman. And she was dreading his making a pass at her because she knew she would not be able to keep quiet if he did that. Her jealousy, her resentment of him, her love for him would cause an indignant, pathetic explosion and then he would know she was crazily, deeply in love with him.

Dawn felt trapped in many ways. She had committed herself to working on the next book with Amelia. So from now until November she must maintain the status quo; she must control herself and her emotions and keep life pleasant all round. At the end of October, before Amelia left for her winter in Bermuda, she would tell her there was no question of her working on yet another book, tell her she wanted a permanent job somewhere in Wales, nearer home.

She managed a smile for Cosmo but shortly after they'd finished their coffee, she went to bed.

Her let her go without further questions, accepting that she was tired but giving her another, searching look as he bade her good night.

Dawn cried a little when she got into bed. She wished fervently that she had not made a commitment to Amelia. But it was too late to change her mind now; it would be terribly unfair to do so, after all her kindness. They had agreed to have just three weeks break before they started the next book—one of which had passed— and Dawn had already mentioned that she was going to stay with her mother for the second and third weeks. After the party there was no reason, no excuse for her to stay in Amelia's house. Not that she needed one. In fact Amelia had tried to talk her out of it, saying, 'But why go home, Dawn? You can rest here just as well as you can rest in Wales.'

Which was true. But it had got to the stage where she really had to get away, had to have a break from Cosmo's company. Two weeks in Wales would probably help to lessen the pain a little, help her to put things in perspective, help her truly to adjust to the knowledge that loving Cosmo Temple was pointless. With all this in mind, she had said to Amelia, simply, 'Yes, but my mum and my aunty have been missing me, you understand.'

On Saturday morning, Dawn woke to find Cosmo sitting on the foot of her bed. For a few seconds she

didn't register where she was when she opened her eyes
... then she became aware instantly that she was not
alone ...

'Cosmo!' Panic stricken, she sat bolt upright,
unwittingly giving him a view of the top half of her
naked body. 'What on earth—what are you doing in
here? What's wrong? What *is* it? Amelia ...?'

'No, no, nothing's wrong. Everything's fine.' He was
sitting perfectly still, naked, presumably, except for the
bath-towel which was tied around his waist. 'I was just
watching you while you slept, that's all. Just thinking
how beautiful you are ...' His eyes trailed to her
breasts, making her aware of her nakedness. 'Very
beautiful.'

She snatched the sheet in front of her, angry with
him. 'You idiot, you frightened the life out of me! Get
out of here!'

He stayed where he was, looking positively hurt, as
though he were perfectly entitled to walk into her room
and watch her sleeping. 'Dawn! How ungrateful you
are. After all the trouble I've been to!'

Her eyes narrowed suspiciously and she had to force
herself not to laugh now. 'What trouble?'

He jerked a thumb downwards and sure enough, on
the low table at the side of her bed was a cup of tea and
a round of toast. 'That's just to keep you going till
breakfast—bacon, eggs, the works!'

All was forgiven! She reached carefully for the tea
and smiled at him. 'Thanks. Give me two minutes to
have this, five minutes to shower and then I'll join you.
Sunny side up for me, please.'

'What?' He got up then.

'My eggs. Sunny side up.' It dawned slowly. 'You did
mean *you* were cooking breakfast, didn't you?'

He looked indignant. 'Oh, come on, darling! There

are limits! I'll give you those seven minutes—in which to get into that kitchen and make me——'

She threw a pillow at him as he laughingly left the room.

It missed.

As she was frying bacon some fifteen minutes later, happy and humming to herself and not minding this in the least, she was reminded of the time when she had gone storming into the kitchens at the Glendale Inn and informed her mother that the man in room twelve wanted *six* slices of bacon for his breakfast. Oh, how long ago that seemed! How much had happened since that morning, how much she loved him now, how much she had learned about him . . .

Her humming stopped and was replaced by a long sigh.

There was the rustle of a newspaper and then Cosmo was by her side, kissing her lightly on the back of the neck. 'Hey, don't be like that! This was just a joke, you know. I'm quite happy to take over the cooking if——'

She couldn't help smiling. He had heard her sigh and had had no idea what was going through her mind. 'Sit down and shut up, Cosmo. You probably wouldn't have the first clue!' She pushed him away, laughing even more because he didn't contradict her.

They had almost finished eating when the door-bell rang. 'Now who the devil . . .?' Cosmo got to his feet, muttering to himself, and Dawn closed her eyes. How was this going to look? Here they were, eating breakfast, both wearing dressing-gowns at . . . she glanced at the clock . . . eleven-thirty in the morning. Anyone would think she was one of his . . . Her eyes flew open in alarm. Dear God, what if it was one of his women?

It was Richie.

Dawn heard his voice and let out a sigh of relief. Richie was already of the opinion that she and Cosmo were lovers—so why worry? He would never be convinced to the contrary, not now!

But Cosmo's love life was the last thing Richie had on his mind. He walked into the kitchen with Cosmo hard on his heels, with Cosmo asking him repeatedly what the hell was the matter with him.

Richie was pale and drawn, the tension in him showing in his every jerky movement. Dawn's heart sank. He had come back from New York just two or three days ago, she knew, but this was more than jet-lag he was suffering from.

Something was terribly wrong.

'Anthea wants a divorce!' The words burst from him as he sank into a chair at the kitchen table. 'This morning, first thing, right out of the blue she tells me she wants a divorce!'

Dawn looked at Cosmo, Cosmo was staring at Richie. The older man's face was hard, unsympathetic. 'Don't be so wet, Richie! You can hardly say it's out of the blue!'

Aghast at his lack of understanding, Dawn couldn't keep quiet. 'Cosmo! Give him . . .'

But Richie didn't seem to have heard. Suddenly he was ranting, furious but obviously deeply upset. 'There was no preamble, nothing! She might just as well have been telling me the sun's shining today. And if you don't mind, *she* wants a divorce! *She's* going to see a solicitor! Anyone would think *she's* the injured party!'

When Cosmo opened his mouth to speak, Dawn gave him a swift kick under the table and glared at him. He shut his mouth, shut his eyes and nodded slowly, collecting himself. 'Give him a cup of tea, Dawn.'

Relieved, she made a fresh pot of tea, and all the time she was doing so Richie was prowling around the kitchen, unable to remain seated, going on and on and on at the way Anthea had just coolly, cold-bloodedly, made her announcement.

When Dawn put the teapot on the table, Richie sat down again, heavily, silent now. For one minute nobody spoke, everything was calm. Richie had blown off his steam and was sitting absolutely still now. Dawn's heart went out to him as she poured him some tea, watching him without appearing to do so. He looked exhausted and he looked too thin. In the past few minutes he seemed to have shrunk slightly inside the clothes he was wearing.

He was staring down at the table, shaking his head as Dawn pushed the cup towards him. 'So what do I do now?' he asked quietly, helplessly. 'I *know* what she is yet I *still* love her. *I still love her!* I must be nuts! Maybe I'll just go out and shoot myself——'

Suddenly the cup of tea was flying from the table, crashing and splattering over the kitchen floor. Dawn squealed in horror, unable to believe what was happening. Cosmo's chair had fallen backwards with a crash as he lunged towards his brother. He reached for Richie's throat, gathering a handful of jumper in the process and now he was shaking the younger man violently, shouting in a voice which was nothing less than vicious. 'If you ever come out with a crack like that again, I'll knock the stuffing out of you! Do you *hear* me, Richard? Have you *got* that?'

Dawn's breathing was suspended. She stared at Cosmo as though she'd never seen him before. Well, she hadn't. Not like this! She couldn't believe her eyes, her ears. It was seconds, long, long seconds before she understood, before she remembered.

It was as if everything had accelerated in time, just for those seconds. Suddenly Cosmo was back in his chair again, his hands raking through his hair, and Richie was staring at him, his face even paler now. And it was Richie who spoke first, Richie's words which made Dawn remember. 'Jesus, Cosmo, I'm sorry! I'm *sorry*! I wasn't thinking—I didn't mean it, I just——'

Oh, God! Dawn called out silently, not knowing what to do, what to say. 'I—I'll just——'

'Stay where you are, Dawn.' Cosmo's command was extremely quiet, was not to be argued with. She sat motionless.

'I'm sorry,' he said to his brother. 'I'm sorry, kid, I just . . .'

'Forget it. I know.' Richie smiled faintly. He turned to Dawn, a look of apology in his eyes because he didn't know that she understood, too. 'I just happened to say the wrong thing, Dawn.'

She nodded, silent.

It was all over. All awkwardness, all temper had fled. Cosmo got up first. 'Come on, let's go into the living room and talk this thing through.'

'No. I—there's no point, Cosmo.' Richie straightened his clothes, got tiredly to his feet. 'I'm going out for a drive.'

'Now listen——'

'No. It's okay, don't worry. I'm not going to do something stupid and I'm not going to get drunk. Believe it or not, I'm coming to terms with it already. As you said, it's hardly out of the blue. Anthea's started the ball rolling because I wouldn't get round to it. But I want to be alone now, if you don't mind. I'll see you at the party tomorrow.' The last remark was for Dawn. She just nodded again because she couldn't think of anything appropriate to say.

'Is Anthea likely to be there,' Cosmo wanted to know, 'at the party?'

Richie shrugged. 'I don't know. I honestly have no idea.'

'Then ask her—tell her—to be there, for Amelia's sake. And neither of you must say a word about the divorce just yet. I don't want anything to spoil Amelia's evening tomorrow.'

Richie let himself out, Cosmo stayed in the kitchen with Dawn. Silence reigned for several minutes, until she could stand it no longer.

'Cosmo . . .'

'I'm sorry.' He interrupted hastily as she shattered his reverie. 'You must wonder what the devil came over me. Perhaps I'd better explain . . .'

'There's no need.' She didn't want him to tell her because he felt obliged to. 'You don't have to explain yourself to me, Cosmo.'

'Of course I do.' He frowned as though she'd said something stupid. 'Besides, this is something I want you to know about . . .'

They did go out, eventually. Just as far as Hyde Park. By then it was the middle of the afternoon and they both wanted a walk in the sun. Cosmo had told her the story about his father in full. Some of the details Amelia remembered, Cosmo did not. Some of the things Cosmo added Amelia had never known, could only have guessed at. Only he could tell of the way he had felt at the time of his father's suicide. And that's what he told Dawn, of his feelings, his thoughts, his fears at the time, of his insecurity, his anger and of the conclusions, decisions, he had come to.

They went out to eat in the evening. Dawn would have been happy to cook for him but she readily agreed with his suggestion that they get dressed up and go somewhere quiet and luxurious.

She had never felt as close to him as she did over dinner that night. When he reached for her hand, there was no question of her pulling away this time. She loved him regardless of—regardless of anything—and she felt honoured that he had trusted her not only with the facts about his father's life but also with his most private thoughts at the time.

Cosmo had no idea she'd heard the story before, of course, had no idea how much thought she'd given to it. Well, it was official now, he'd told her everything himself, and there were several things she wanted to say to him on the matter, but she waited until they were back in the privacy of his flat.

Thomas wasn't around so it was Cosmo who poured a nightcap for them. 'Brandy, Dawn?'

'I'd love one.' She made herself comfortable in an armchair, hoping he wouldn't resent the things she was about to say to him. But it was important, she had to talk to him about his attitudes, about the effect his father's suicide had had on him. 'Cosmo, I—I've been giving a lot of thought to the things you told me today, about your father and the way you felt at the time . . .'

She began tentatively and she was encouraged by the way he listened. She talked to him at some length but Cosmo made hardly any comment. He just—listened, his face impassive throughout.

Later, when he kissed her good night, he did so tenderly. But it was, she realised, merely a kiss of gratitude. For her interest. For her show of concern. Whether voicing her opinion had actually done any good or not, she couldn't tell.

CHAPTER TWELVE

'I HAVE the strangest feeling that you're up to something, Cosmo!' Amelia looked suspiciously at her nephew as they all climbed into a taxi. Cosmo's flat was in easy walking distance of the hotel and they could have strolled there comfortably since it was such a beautiful evening. But that wasn't part of the plan.

Dawn, Mrs Watt and the Major exchanged smiles while Cosmo said he had no idea what his aunt was talking about. Just a few minutes later she was saying, 'I say! Dinner at the Dorchester, is it? How very nice, Cosmo! Richie and Anthea are meeting us here, I take it?'

Dawn shot a quick look at Cosmo as they got out of the taxi. She certainly hoped so. She hoped that Anthea would turn up for Amelia's sake, for Richie's sake. And for Cosmo, too, who had put so much effort into this evening.

Richie was in fact on the look-out at the hotel and Dawn caught a glimpse of him as he vanished on seeing their arrival. It was his job to see that the lights were off as Cosmo opened the door to the reception room ...

It worked beautifully. Amelia was ushered through the door first and as she was greeted by a darkened room, there was just time for her, 'I think you've made a mistake, Cosmo ...' And then suddenly the lights were on, a sea of faces was smiling at her and the band was playing 'For She's a Jolly Good Fellow ...'

Dawn would never forget the picture that was Amelia's face, nor the story it told. She was stunned, bewildered, a little over-awed, and yes, she was delighted. Her soft, brown eyes were brilliant with tears. She turned to Cosmo, unable to speak, just grabbing hold of his arm as if for support. Major Wright was by her side, too, beaming all over his face and murmuring, 'Come, come now, my dear . . .'

'Oh, Eustace! Cosmo . . . Richie . . .'

They were all kissing her, hugging her, congratulating her not only on reaching three score years and ten but also for being the person she was, for her achievements, for the pleasure she had given to millions of children during the past twenty years or more.

Anthea wasn't there.

Had she been there, she would have been at Richie's side. Jeremy appeared to be alone, too, which was something of a surprise. Cosmo had invited one hundred and nineteen people to the party and from the look of things everyone had turned up. Promptly, too.

Except Anthea.

It was an unforgettable, wonderful evening. For the first hour or so the music from the band was subdued, serving only as a background to the hubbub of chatter as people drank, nibbled delicious little titbits offered by the waiters who were doing a splendid job. Dawn chatted and circulated, as did everyone else, meeting people familiar and unfamiliar to her.

The party had started early and it was only nine o'clock when the doors to the adjoining room were opened. It was in this room that the buffet was being served—and Cosmo had spared no expense. There was everything one could think of to eat—and more— from Russina caviare to cold pheasant.

Dawn had fifteen minutes with Cosmo while they ate and she congratulated him on the success of the party. The atmosphere was wonderful, happy, gay and celebratory. From the main reception room came the music from the band, louder now as people started to dance. She did not mention Anthea's name.

Jeremy mentioned Anthea's name.

It was about half an hour later, while she was dancing with him. Cosmo was nowhere tò be seen at that point and Richie was dancing with a pretty redhead who worked for Amelia's publisher.

'I'm disappointed.' Jeremy's arms were lightly around Dawn and she saw the wicked smile on his face.

'At what? Not the party, surely?'

'Of course not. At the fact that Anthea isn't here. I would have found it very entertaining indeed.'

Dawn had no idea what he meant. Surely—surely he hadn't heard about the divorce, not so quickly? She looked around anxiously, her eyes searching for Amelia; she and the Major were sitting down, their heads together as if in consultation. But there was a smile on Amelia's face so there was nothing to worry about.

Shaking her head slightly, Dawn sighed resignedly. 'You've heard, then?' He had, it was obvious.

'Are you kidding? I should think it's common knowledge by now!'

She looked at him sadly, her eyes appealing. 'Isn't it awful, the way people gossip?'

Jeremy seemed amused. 'It's their own fault. If they'd wanted to keep it a secret, they should have used more integrity.' He glanced over at Richie. 'As is usually the case—the husband is the last to know. He hasn't a clue, but that won't last much longer, surely?'

Dawn's mouth open and closed. 'I don't—Jeremy, what *are* you talking about?'

'Oh, come on, Dawn! I'm talking about the affair Anthea's having with Cosmo.'

She stopped dancing, unable to take it in. 'What? *What?*'

Jeremy stared at her, swearing softly. 'You mean you didn't know? But you just—I thought——' He pulled her into his arms again, dismissing the subject as if it didn't matter. But Dawn was like a piece of wood in his arms and when he saw how white her face had gone, he immediately led her off the dance floor. 'What on earth's the matter with you, Dawn?' Then at her silence, at her whiteness, 'Oh, for God's sake ... *you* haven't fallen for him, have you? I warned you ages ago what he was like, what a womaniser he is!'

'You're wrong!' Dawn's ears were ringing; she was shocked to the core, furious with him. 'How dare you! How can you! Cosmo is Richie's brother, for God's sake!'

'Stranger things happen at sea, my dear.' He wasn't in the least perturbed, he was actually amused! 'And in my profession, let me assure you——'

'I don't want to hear about your profession! And I don't want to hear——' She stopped. Her voice had risen and a couple of people turned to look at her. The awful, unforgivable thing was ... that she couldn't dismiss this as being a total lie. Why should Jeremy lie? He might not care much for Cosmo but he didn't hate the man. And besides, there was Richie and—no, it was too *awful*!

'Come on.' Jeremy put a firm hand under her elbow and steered her from the room. They turned a corner at the end of the corridor and he led her to a small, elegant chaise longue. 'Sit down, Dawn. Look—didn't you know that Anthea knew Cosmo before she met Richie? That she had a thing going with big brother before she married Richie?'

'I—well—yes. I knew, I knew *something* about it.' She had known some of it—but not all of it. She had believed Cosmo when he'd said there had been nothing between him and Anthea, when he'd said he had made a point of telling Richie this on the eve of his wedding.

She felt dizzy. Surely this couldn't be true? Surely Cosmo's words to his brother had not been deliberately ambiguous? Or maybe he hadn't said them at all? Richie hadn't mentioned it ... 'Jeremy, Jeremy, this is important. I must know. Are you *sure*?'

'That they had an affair or that they're having one?'

'Either. Both.'

'I'm sure.' He shrugged, not seeing what the fuss was about. 'Have you met Anthea? Dawn, that girl just *oozes* sex——'

That was true. She knew that much; she could understand why a man would make such a remark. But that wasn't enough to convince her—'Never mind that. I'm talking about *facts*. All right, maybe they had an affair in the past, but why on earth should you think it's still going on?'

'Well, for one thing I saw them out together only last week.'

Dawn still couldn't believe it, still wouldn't give up. 'Are you sure? Where? When, exactly? Could you have been mistaken?'

Jeremy laughed openly. 'My, you are easily shockable, aren't you? Who could mistake Cosmo? Or Anthea? Put the two together and you've got a very striking couple, to say the least. It was in a wine bar in Richmond.' He grinned. 'Which is rather out of the way, don't you think? Somewhere they didn't think they'd be seen?'

Dawn felt as though all the strength were seeping slowly out of her body. Last week, he'd said, while Richie was in New York ...

'It was last Wednesday, just four days ago. I remember what day it was because I'd been over at Shepperton Studios ... anyhow, neither of them saw me. I spotted them straight away, sitting in a corner, heads together. They left after I'd been there two minutes, before I'd even got myself a drink. I was so entertained that I followed them. I got into my car and followed them right into town, to Cosmo's flat which is just across——'

'Excuse me.' Dawn got unsteadily to her feet. 'Jeremy, please go back into the party. I'll be along shortly.'

'As you like. Hey, not a word about this——'

'And that goes for you, too.' She almost spat at him. She hated him for telling her what she knew could be the truth. Somewhere deep inside her, she knew it could be the truth. Jeremy had no motive for lying. And there were other things, too, other things which Dawn remembered . . .

She went into the ladies room, locked herself in a lavatory and was physically sick. When she emerged, she splashed cold water on her cheeks, rinsed her mouth out and sat down, grateful she was alone in there. Her mind was racing frantically, remembering things and still, *still*, trying to explain them away.

Echoes of Anthea's voice were going round in her head. Clearly now she remembered the conversation she had heard that day at Cornerways. '. . . Coffee? Black, without sugar, if I remember correctly . . .' Dawn had thought nothing of this, had thought that as Cosmo's sister-in-law, Anthea would know how he liked his coffee. But it had been said jokingly, teasingly, and could so easily have been the words of one lover to another probably said with a smile.

'. . . It's over. Face it.' Those words had been from Cosmo, and Dawn had thought they referred to Anthea's marriage—but they might have referred to their affair. Had he been in the throes of finishing it? Was that why Anthea had come to take a look at

Dawn? And that had been her reason for visiting that day. She'd said as much. So had Cosmo's conscience started troubling him? Or maybe the affair had started soon after that? *Resumed* after that. Because Cosmo couldn't resist her. Anthea had always wanted him. Richie had said so.

In spite of everything, Dawn tried desperately to explain it away, all of it, even Richie's saying to Anthea that he knew she never saw her lover at week ends. Because of this, Richie had assumed her lover was a married man. Had Cosmo and Anthea agreed not to see one another at week ends, deliberately, as a red-herring? To make Richie reach the conclusion he had reached?

It couldn't be true! Not *this*. Not *Cosmo*. Yet Dawn couldn't deny the impossibility of Jeremy mistaking them for someone else when he'd seen them out together. And he had followed them back into London. But he couldn't have seen them actually going into Cosmo's flat. He couldn't have, not when it was on the top floor of a building. All right, maybe he'd seen Cosmo park his car ... maybe Cosmo had wanted to talk to Anthea about something while—while Richie was away ...? No, that didn't hold water. It was no use. This couldn't be explained away ...

And so it went on. Dawn was absent from the party for over half an hour. But when she went back she got all the confirmation she needed.

Cosmo was hovering near the door. He took hold of her arm as soon as she appeared. 'Dawn, you look so white! Are you ill? I was just about to send someone to search for you——'

She didn't even have the strength to shake his hand from her arm. 'It's—just the rich food. I'm okay now.'

He seemed genuinely concerned, but Dawn had got

to the pitch where she felt that she didn't really know this man at all. He wanted her physically, she knew that, and he had lied to her in an effort to persuade her into doing something she didn't want to do. That *was* the top and bottom of it. And this knowledge made it easier to believe he was actually living a lie, was a traitor to his own brother.

'Good,' he said, still holding on to her. 'Because you're just in time for——'

He was interrupted by the band striking up with 'Happy Birthday To You', and in came the birthday cake. It was precisely eleven o'clock and the cake was wheeled in on a beautifully decorated trolley, a three-tier cake with elaborate icing and seventy candles.

One person and then another called for a speech. Cosmo excused himself and left Dawn's side. He went on to the platform where the band was, as did Richie, and together they said a few words about their aunt, wishing her health and happiness for many years to come, thanking her for all she had done for them, all she meant to them.

As this went on Dawn became aware of someone standing behind her. She was still near the door and suddenly the hair on the back of her neck was bristling, as if she knew . . .

She turned to see Anthea, who shot her a quick, cool smile of recognition. The older girl looked magnificent, her low-cut, white satin dress putting Dawn's pale blue chiffon in the shade, making her feel gauche and unsophisticated.

Dawn's eyes flicked over her slowly, sadly, and when her gaze took in the details of Anthea's face, her upswept hair, she knew that there was no mistake, that she could make no more excuses, that she could not explain away what Jeremy had told her. For Anthea was wearing a pair of exquisite ear-rings, ear-rings made from tiny pearls surrounded by chips of diamond.

That was the strangest moment of Dawn's life. It was a moment of devastating panic combined with the utmost clarity. Incongruously, ridiculously, she caught herself thinking how surprising it was that one of those ear-rings had not, after all, ended up in a vacuum-cleaner. Her head was throbbing again, her heart accelerating so fast that she thought she would faint. The ear-ring, one of *these* ear-rings, had been on the floor of Cosmo's bedroom not *last* week but the week *before* . . . And Richie had been away all that time.

There was no mistake.

There was no reason to doubt Jeremy any longer, no more excuses to be found. *Cosmo was the man with whom Anthea was having an affair.*

Dawn turned around to see that Amelia was on the platform now. She watched the old lady standing shyly, happily, her hand outstretched to Major Wright as she urged him on to the platform with her. Their combined speech was heard by Dawn as well as everyone else. The difference was that Dawn had to remind herself to look pleased, that she ought to be pleased. But although she was hearing the words from the two people on the platform, they weren't really registering with her . . .

'. . . And I, or rather we,' Amelia was saying, 'have a surprise for *you*, which I think is only fair after—all this!' She lost her courage then, was daunted by the dozens of people watching her, listening intently. 'Perhaps Eustace had better say it for me——'

Major Wright didn't know what shyness was. Loudly, proudly, he got straight to the point. 'Amelia and I would like to take this opportunity of announcing our engagement. We shall be married this year, during the first week of November!'

There was applause, there were gasps of surprise and delight. Dawn's eyes moved of their own volition to the other men on the platform, to Richie and Cosmo. Then someone was touching her arm and an amused, female voice was saying, 'Yes, I suppose it is touching, isn't it?'

Only then was Dawn aware of the tears rolling down her cheeks.

Then there was another voice, Jeremy's. 'And what would you know, Anthea darling? You've never been emotionally touched by anything in your entire life. Except, perhaps, Cosmo.'

There was laughter. 'Why don't you keep your big mouth shut, Jeremy?'

Dawn moved away from them, wondering how she was going to live through the remainder of the evening.

But that wasn't as difficult as she imagined it would be. When the party broke up at the Dorchester, a smaller one continued in Cosmo's flat. This was just for the family and those closest to Amelia, which included her publisher of so many years.

Amelia spoke of her plans to retire after she had fulfilled her commitments, her next book. It was to be her last. She and the Major were going to live permanently in Bermuda, in the sun . . .

Anthea was there, drinking champagne, her eyes almost constantly on Cosmo, but there was so much chatter from others, so much happening that Dawn was able to cope satisfactorily. Also, an icy calm had come over her; it was as though she were immune to everything and anyone—even the sight of Anthea and Cosmo and the deceit which was, they thought, their secret.

When the Major left to go home with his son for the night, Dawn excused herself and went to bed even before Amelia did. In the morning the Major was coming back to drive her, Dawn and Mrs Watt back to Cornerways.

Dawn went into the blue guest room and sat for a long time, staring at nothing. She was so utterly, totally calm, she couldn't believe it herself.

She was just grateful for it.

CHAPTER THIRTEEN

'ARE you sure you feel up to it, dear? I mean, after last night's party and the drive down here today—why don't you leave it till tomorrow?' Amelia was looking at her worriedly.

Dawn's bags were packed and she couldn't wait to get away, from this house, from anything and anyone associated with Cosmo. And that even included Amelia. 'I'll be fine, don't worry. I'll give you a ring to let you know I've arrived safely in Wales.'

Home. What she should have said was 'arrived safely at home'. But this house had become home to her, this house which she was now desperate to get out of. It was all so confusing, really, so clear and yet so utterly, painfully, confusing. She hadn't known, before, what it felt like when the bottom of one's world drops out.

In no danger of crying, she said a warm farewell to Amelia and Mrs Watt. She knew she would not be coming back to Cornerways, but she couldn't tell Amelia yet. Not yet. Amelia must have a happy day today, to enjoy the aftermath of the party and the astonishing announcement she'd made. She must not be allowed to worry over things which did not concern her.

Dawn knew exactly what she was going to do. As she drove home she went over her plans again. She would telephone Amelia in a few days time and explain that her mother needed her help at the inn, now that it was July and the busiest part of the season.

What she couldn't do was let Amelia down. Not at such short notice. Therefore, she would tell her that they would have to work separately on the book, Amelia at Cornerways as usual, Dawn in Wales. They could communicate by post. It wouldn't be quite as convenient, and nothing like as pleasant for either of them, but it would be more than satisfactory as far as the book was concerned because Dawn was very familiar with Amelia's method of working by now.

Never, ever again did she want to set eyes on Cosmo.

And yet, even knowing what he was, she still loved him. She knew now how Richie felt. Maybe it would take a year, maybe it would take the rest of her life for her to get over this. This foolishness.

It had taken Amelia many, many years to get over the death of the man she loved. Last night's announcement, when it had finally registered with Dawn, had been a surprise indeed.

But at that stage in life, she knew Amelia's marriage to Major Wright would be mostly for companionship. Amelia herself had said, about her lost love, 'Life rarely gives anyone that kind of love twice.'

That's how it would be for Dawn.

She was desperate to get to Wales. Shirley would understand. Aunty Megan might, too. She did not intend to tell them the facts, what she had been through and what she was going through. She couldn't talk about it, wouldn't talk about it. But they would have some suspicions, naturally. Still, they wouldn't pry. They would leave her to her own devices and not ask questions if she wanted to stay in her room for a few days.

She had to get over her feelings for Cosmo. She had to start doing that *now*.

If he telephoned her, she knew exactly what she would say to him.

It was dinner time when she pulled up on the car park at the back of the Glendale Inn. The car park was almost full. At this time of year there was a lot of passing trade, most especially in this weather. That meant that the bar would be full, the dining room likewise. Everyone would be busy, everyone would be entertained, so she could get into the private quarters without questions from Miss Williams or anyone else.

At least for tonight.

Fond though she was of her old teacher, Dawn realised she would have to avoid her company for a few days. She couldn't face her curiosity. Not yet. For as calm as she was, deep though this calmness went inside her, she could not trust herself not to cry if someone happened to say the wrong thing.

It was rather like sitting on a time-bomb.

Of course it would pass. Wouldn't it? Time was, they said, the great healer.

A few days later, Shirley reminded her daughter that she hadn't yet told Amelia she was not going back to the New Forest. Dawn said she would ring the next day, but the next day was Friday and in the middle of the morning there was a delivery of flowers for her. It was a beautiful bouquet of two dozen roses and with them there was a card bearing a message from Cosmo: 'I miss you. Happy holiday—but hurry home.'

Without the slightest trace of emotion, Dawn dropped the card and the flowers into the litter bin. Cosmo Temple was a liar and a hypocrite, and even while he was conducting an affair with Anthea, he was still pursuing what he wanted from Dawn! How right Jeremy had been in saying he was a womaniser!

So she made her call to Amelia on the following Tuesday, when she knew there was no danger of Cosmo being at Cornerways, no danger of his answering the 'phone.

After five minutes of explanations and the exchange of news, Amelia said, 'Well, yes, of course we can work like that. But tell me the truth, is something wrong?'

'I'm needed here, Amelia.' Dawn did her best not to lie, to avoid the question. 'The season's in full swing now and it will be until the end of August. It's a question of an extra pair of hands, you see, especially during the evening.'

Dawn had been working, too. She hadn't stayed in her room, after all. She'd cleaned, she'd worked in the bar, on reception—on anything which would take her mind off Cosmo. But it didn't help much, and with every passing day more and more tension was building inside her. The time-bomb was getting nearer and nearer to exploding.

What hurt most of all was the disillusionment. With him, with herself. What a complete and utter fool she had been in falling for a man like that! But how did one stop it, how did one fall *out* of love? Work was the only solution she could think of. Work, work and more work.

For the rest of the week, Dawn continued to do just that. She worked herself into a state of exhaustion until, early on Friday evening, her mother finally put her foot down.

'All right, Dawn, that's enough! Come in here, I want to talk to you.' Shirley took the cleaning cloth and the bottle of brass polish from her daughter's hands and jerked her head in the direction of the living room. Once they were seated, she came straight out with it: 'What's going on, exactly? What's happened between you and Cosmo that's so awful you can't face him again?'

Dawn looked down at her hands. There was no point in denying that Cosmo had something to do with this, her mother was not a stupid woman. Far from it. 'Mum, I don't want to talk about it. I—can't. At least, not yet.'

Patiently, Shirley took hold of her hand. 'Dawn, I can't say I know how you feel, because I never suffered like this when I fell in love with your father. I've never experienced what you're going though—apart from mourning him, which isn't quite the same thing. Not quite, but that misery and the misery you're going through are close enough to enable me at least to understand. You're in love with Cosmo, but he doesn't feel the same way. It's the only conclusion I can reach. Now, I don't mind your working off your unhappiness, Dawn, but I'm not going to stand by and watch you make yourself ill. You look worn out, don't you realise that? And for another thing——'

She was interrupted by the shrill ring of the telephone and she got up reluctantly, loath to break off this conversation.

A moment later she had her hand clamped over the telephone receiver and she was smiling at Dawn. 'It's him! Cosmo! He wants to talk to you.'

Dawn shared none of her mother's pleasure. Coldly, ruthlessly, she asked her mother to make an excuse. 'Tell him I'm in the bath, tell him I'm not here. Tell him anything. But I won't talk to him.'

'This is silly, Dawn. He'll only ring back——'

'No. I don't think so. He'll take the hint.'

Shirley did as she was asked but a moment later she was covering the receiver again, having difficulty suppressing a smile. 'It's no use. He's just told me I'm lying! He saw right through me, Dawn! Now come on, I'll leave you in private . . .' And with that, she put the receiver on the sideboard and left the room.

'Oh, God . . .' With a groan, Dawn got up. She might as well get this over with. 'Hello?'

'Dawn! What's going on? Why are you trying to avoid me?' He sounded cross, very cross, and he gave her no chance to answer. 'I've just got to Amelia's. I expected to find you here, I expected you back today. Instead I've been greeted with the news that you're not coming back *at all*! Now what the hell is going on? And don't try giving *me* that rubbish about your mother needing your help because I just won't swallow it!'

Dawn looked at the receiver, unmoved by his outburst. 'Dawn?' She could hear him shouting at her now. 'Dawn, what's wrong?'

She almost smiled. *What's wrong?* Everything in the world was wrong! She didn't say another word. Very calmly, without the slightest trace of emotion, without any qualms, she put the receiver back on its cradle.

She owed Cosmo Temple *nothing*, not even an explanation.

The 'phone did not ring again.

CHAPTER FOURTEEN

DAWN really was in the bath when Cosmo arrived that night. It was almost eleven o'clock when Shirley hammered on the door and called to her. 'Dawn? Dawn! It's Cosmo. He's here!'

Dawn pulled herself swiftly into a sitting position, slopping water over the side of the bath as all her calm suddenly disintegrated. '*Here?* At the inn?'

'Yes, you idiot. He's in the living room and your Aunty Megan's looking very confused. He's absolutely furious and——'

'I won't see him!'

'*What?*'

'You heard me.' Her voice was rising, panicky. 'Tell him—tell him to go away. Just *go away.*'

'Dawn! Darling, I think you'd better hear what he has to say. In fact, I think you have no choice . . .'

Shirley was right, of course. There was no chance of his going away, just like that. He had driven for hours in order to see her and there was no chance of that now, none at all. Cosmo was not a man to be thwarted. With a sigh of resignation, she told her mother she would be out of the bathroom in five minutes.

Drying herself quickly, she went into her bedroom and slipped on a full-length towelling robe. She was trembling; all her composure had deserted her. The knowledge that he was here was more than enough to have that effect on her, and that alone made her angry. But it was nothing compared to the anger she felt towards him, the resentment. The time-bomb was about

to explode and she only hoped that her mother and her
aunt had had the tact to make themselves scarce.

They had. Cosmo was alone in the living room, was
standing by the sideboard, still wearing the suit he'd
worn to the office that day. By his side was an
untouched drink. That was Shirley's idea, no doubt,
something to calm him down while he waited . . .

But he didn't appear to be furious, not now. Had he
been, Dawn might have coped better, she might have
kept her dignity instead of hissing at him through
clenched teeth. 'Get out of here, Cosmo. Can't you
take a hint? I don't want to talk to you!'

'I gathered that.' He was smiling, actually smiling!
'What I want to know is—why not?'

The bomb went off at that instant. 'Because you're a
liar and a cheat! Because you're an immoral, traitorous,
despicable—*bastard*!'

Beneath the tan of his skin, he paled. He had, at
least, the good grace to look horrified. Dawn lunged
ahead with her accusations right then, while he was
wide open to her attack. 'You thought I didn't know,
didn't you? Well I've got news for you, half of London
knows about the affair you're having with Anthea.
Except, of course, for Richie! And how long do you
think you can keep it from him? How can you *do* this?
How could you do it to your own *brother*? Hasn't he
been through enough without learning what kind of
man *you* are?'

She had said it. All of it. And now she was exhausted.
All the pent-up emotion, not only of the past two weeks
in Wales but also of the months of loving him, came
bursting to the surface and she sank into a chair, head
in hands, and sobbed.

It was quite a while before Cosmo came near her,
before she felt the firm grip of his hands on her wrists.

He pulled her to her feet, tried to take her in his arms, but she thrashed out at him hysterically, beating her hands against his chest. 'Get away from me. Get *away*!'

Still he didn't speak. She had time enough to see that the colour had not returned to his face, that he was rigid with tension, before he put both arms around her in a vice-like grip. He held her tightly against him, stroking her hair, soothing her. 'Dawn, Dawn, listen to me. You're *wrong*. For God's sake, you've got to believe me. You're *wrong*! I am not having, I never have had, an affair with Anthea. I can't imagine how you've got this idea into your head. I'm appalled. Not with you, but with the person who's been gossiping to you. Who, Dawn? Who is it?'

She tried to pull away from him but he wouldn't let her. Helplessly she stared at him, not believing him. 'You're lying, Cosmo! You lied when you said you loved me and you're lying now! Jeremy Wright——'

'*Jeremy!* What? What has he said to you? Dear God, Dawn, don't you know by now what a gossip he is? He's as much a bitch as my sister-in-law—the male equivalent!'

'No, Cosmo, not this time, he isn't!' She wanted to believe him. Oh, how she desperately wanted to believe him but ... but the evidence was too much to be explained away. She had tried that, she had tried very hard indeed to do that.

She started talking, accusing, almost babbling, telling him firstly about the ear-ring in his bedroom then switching to Jeremy's sighting him with Anthea in the wine bar. The next minute, she was going on about the conversation she had accidentally overheard in Cornerways, the conversation between him and Anthea. But Cosmo didn't interrupt her, not once. He let her pour it all out, listening, frowning, intent on her every word even as she jumped back and forth in time. She told him of the short conversation between Jeremy and Anthea at the party, how Anthea hadn't denied Jeremy's remark about her feelings for Cosmo, but had merely told him to keep his mouth shut, how she had laughed. And the next thing, she was saying how Anthea never saw her lover at the weekend, as Richie had pointed out . . .

'Is that it?' Unsmiling, deeply concerned, Cosmo looked straight into her eyes when she had talked herself dry. She nodded, her heart pounding in her breast because she hadn't expected this reaction from him. Quite what she had expected, she didn't know, but not this—this total calm. Further, she realised it was just a veneer. In fact he was extremely upset, and even before he began his explanation, she started to feel guilty.

'Dawn, sit down. Sit down and tell me everything all over again, in some semblance of order this time. And when you've finished, it will be your turn to listen . . .'

She did as he asked, slowly, quietly, and even as she retold her tale, she was again seeing possible explanations for some things. For some, but not all. The wine bar, that was an eye-witness account. And the ear-ring, the ear-ring in his bedroom, there could be no acceptable explanation for *that*. God knows she had tried to find one!

But she loved him. She loved him helplessly, hopelessly, regardless, and she listened to him with the faint hope that he might somehow convince her she was wrong.

Cosmo seemed unsure where to begin. He stood, thinking, ordering his thoughts . . . or was he concocting more lies? But Dawn said nothing, she just sat down and waited.

'Richie has a key to my flat, just for emergencies—you know. He obviously didn't take it to New York with him because Anthea used it the first week he was away. I got home late on the Wednesday, the *first* week he was away, note, after an evening out with some clients.'

He looked at her pointedly. 'That's what most of it's about, the social life Jeremy mentioned to you, entertaining clients. It's business, and I assure you it can get very boring at times, Dawn.' He sighed. 'Anyhow, I got home around midnight on the Wednesday and I found Anthea in my flat—in my *bed*, to be precise ...' He registered Dawn's look of astonishment, or disbelief, and went on. 'It's the truth, Dawn. She was naked, she wasn't drunk but she was certainly tipsy. I've no idea where she'd been that evening but she can't have been in the flat long because Thomas would have seen her or heard her. He was in, but he goes to bed around eleven, if I'm out.

'Naturally I was surprised but I can't honestly say I was shocked. Not at her; I know what she is, and she's always made it plain that she's mine for the taking anytime I like.' He looked at her apologetically. 'That's what the conversation at Cornerways was about. Well, partly. I was referring to her marriage when I told her it was over, that she should face it. But all the time I was talking to her, she was flirting with me—hence my remark that she was knocking at a closed door. That referred to *us*, to what she wanted of me.'

Dawn shrugged; she couldn't blame Anthea for fancying Cosmo, couldn't blame her for *that*... 'And how did you react to this—surprise? When you found her in your bed?'

'I didn't even go past the bedroom door. I just held it open and told her to get out. Maybe I should have done this long ago, told her that a woman who throws herself at a man is the worst kind of turn-off I can imagine. Anyway, I told her then ... rather more bluntly, too. She got out of bed and just stood there for a minute, giving me the benefit of seeing all her—attributes. I tell you, Dawn, I was so bloody angry with her, I couldn't say any more. I wanted to throttle her. She *is* beautiful, physically, I've never denied that. And she knows it; she was vain enough not to believe what I'd told her, and she just laughed, *laughed*, and said I should let her know if I ever changed my mind.

'The moment she left, I picked up the 'phone and dialled Richie in New York. I told him what I'd found in my bed. I had to do that, Dawn. Richie's always had his doubts about me and Anthea, about the past, I mean, despite what I told him on the eve of his wedding. I rang him because I was aware that if someone saw her leave my place, or if someone had seen her arrive ... some *gossip* ... it could get back to Richie.'

Some gossip. Dawn hardly knew what to say. She was thinking about Jeremy, about the timing of all this, but mainly she was thinking of poor Richie .... 'How—what did Richie say?'

'He turned on me, would you believe it? He actually accused me of lying about it! I was furious. Oh, he didn't accuse me of making love to his wife, he simply refused to believe she'd been there! He said, "How do I *know* she was there? You'll be a happy man when we end up in the divorce courts, won't you, Cosmo? Is this something you've conjured up to make that happen faster? Maybe you think you're helping, but you're not! Keep out of it, Cosmo. I don't want to hear this."'

'Oh, Lord ...' Dawn shook her head sadly. This, she did believe. She could well imagine Richie wanting to turn a blind eye, to go on fooling himself as he'd been fooling himself for so long. She looked at Cosmo questioningly, imagining his anger at his brother's stupidity, his unfairness.

'As I say, Dawn, it was my turn to be angry. I couldn't believe he thought I'd lied. Basically, deep-down, he didn't believe that, of course. But I didn't stop to think about that at the time.

'His reaction was all part of his ostrich-like attitude. For months he'd buried his head in the sand, refused to do anything about Anthea. He'd been living a lie, living with her, telling himself she'd get over her affairs, that she would stop doing this to him. *Ha!* And in the meantime, he'd drink himself into a stupor every night. I knew it was only a matter of time before he started drinking during the day, before he became incapable even of working. Well, I'd had *enough* of it. I wasn't going to sit around and watch him slowly kill himself over the likes of her. Nor was I going to be accused—or even suspected—of contributing to her infidelities. So, the following week, I rang Richie and got him back from New York a day early. He was due to come home on the Thursday and I told him he had to get back on the Wednesday. I told him something very urgent had cropped up in the business and that I needed him. I knew what time he'd arrive on the Wednesday evening, and I asked him to come straight to my flat. I knew also that he wouldn't bother to let Anthea know he was coming back early—that sort of communication died between them a long time ago.'

Cosmo's anger had resurfaced. Dawn could see it, was very glad it wasn't directed at her.

'*I* 'phoned Anthea, however,' he went on. He looked at Dawn without apology. 'I 'phoned her and told her

I'd had a change of heart. Laughingly I told her she'd won, that I wanted to take her up on her—invitation.' He was smiling now but there was no humour in it. 'She walked straight into my trap without a moment's hesitation. We made a date to meet in the wine bar, which was where I'd first met her a couple of years ago, an out of the way place in Richmond. There, I suggested we would be better having dinner in my flat, that it would be wiser not to be seen out together in London—and off we went.

'Richie was in the flat. He'd been there just ten minutes, according to Thomas. I'd timed it very nicely.'

Dawn was staring at him, imagining Richie's shock when Cosmo had walked in with Anthea. 'Dear God, what a shock he must have had!'

'No! *She* had a shock, which was just what I wanted. Her reaction on seeing Richie was all he needed by way of proof, inescapable proof. Anthea's reaction made it obvious she'd thought she was coming into an empty flat with me. Then, right in front of Richie, I handed her an ear-ring which I'd found on the floor in my bedroom. It was one of a pair Richie had given her on their wedding anniversary.'

Only then did Cosmo sit down. He did not look triumphant, he looked unhappy. 'Anthea left then— after a few choice words to me. But you know, even those were said with laughter. She didn't even have the grace to be humiliated. She simply laughed and walked out. She is, make no mistake, a first class *bitch*.'

'And Richie? How—what——'

'He resented what I'd done. Would you believe it? *Even then*, he tried to explain it away. At that point I wiped the floor with him. I told him how pathetic he was, how Anthea and dozens of other people were laughing at him because he was the only one who refused to acknowledge what he was married to.' He sighed wearily, his fingers raking through the dark curls of his hair. 'It didn't last, his resentment of me, I mean. Fortunately. He knows I'm on his side, that I always have been. And he couldn't blame me for defending myself against his—suspicions. He's asked me now if he can go and work in the office we're in the process of setting up in New York, a branch of the London business. Amelia's been told of the divorce and——'

'And how did she take the news?'

'Well, she wasn't exactly surprised. She was very sad about it, of course, but not exactly surprised. She's always . . . Dawn? What is it?'

Dawn couldn't stop her tears this time, not this time. She owed him an apology, she was aware of that but all she could think of was the hopelessness of her situation, the hopelessness of loving him. Anthea's treatment of his brother was yet another confirmation to Cosmo of the worthlessness of women . . .

He was on his feet now, crossing over to her. Quickly she got up from the settee and kept a distance from him, hardly able to look him in the eye. 'I owe you an apology, Cosmo, and before you go, I want to say——'

'Go?' He seemed at a loss to understand her. 'I'm not going anywhere, not without you. I'm taking you back to Cornerways. I'm taking you *home*. Tonight.'

She sighed, feeling exhausted, and she turned her back to him because she didn't want him to see the tears rolling silently down her face. 'No, no you're not,' she said wearily. 'I am home. Cosmo, I—I'm desperately sorry for believing—about you and Anthea. I should be the first one to realise that things are so often not what they seem.' She kept her back to him, the tears streaming down her cheeks. 'Anthea thought you and I were lovers, did you know that? Not that it made any difference to her——'

'Forget Anthea.' He caught hold of her shoulders and turned her round to face him. 'What about *us*?'

'Us?' She was still avoiding his eyes. 'There's no such thing, Cosmo.'

'The hell——' He shook her. 'Look at me. Look at me, Dawn! I love you. I love you, Dawn! Doesn't that count for anything?'

'Cosmo, please, I—I want you to go now.'

'Don't lie to me!' he said angrily. 'For heaven's sake, don't let's waste any more of our lives with lies and misunderstandings!'

'Our . . . what do you mean?'

Very softly, he said, 'I mean, I'm asking you to marry me.'

Dawn heard the words. Quietly though they'd been spoken, she heard them. She just couldn't believe what she'd heard. 'M-marry? *Marry?* You? I—I——'

He smiled down at her. She looked so aghast, so dumbstruck that he couldn't help smiling. 'Well don't just stand there staring at me, woman. Say something!'

She did. 'No. *No!*'

Suddenly he was roaring with laughter, shaking her again, his grey-black eyes sparkling with amusement. 'Why you crazy little fool! You don't think I'll take that for an answer? I suppose the next thing is you'll be denying you're in love with me!'

'I——' But Dawn got no further. He was kissing her and she was melting against him, clinging to him in the hope that she wasn't dreaming, that he meant what he'd said. All this, she was hoping, but she didn't really think it would be so. It was too—too incredible.

'I want you, Dawn. I want you to——'

'Cosmo, *don't*. Don't do this to me!' Stupidly she had

allowed herself to hope—and now disappointment was almost crushing the breath from her. How stupid, how stupid could she get? Well, she just couldn't take any more. Bravely, she looked at him, and the fact that her heart was reflected in her eyes didn't matter. 'I love you, Cosmo. I've loved you for a long time. So please, don't—what I'm trying to say is that you don't have to marry me to ... I'll go away with you. Tonight, this minute, if that's all you really want ...'

Her words didn't annoy him. He couldn't blame her for this reaction, *this* doubt. Very gently he took hold of her hands and led her to the settee. 'Now listen and don't interrupt. Your future husband is far more realistic than you, in some ways. If all I'd wanted of you was your body, I could have had that long ago. You must know that, if you'll only admit it. But I loved you too much to coax you into something your principles stood against. I love you for those principles, you goose. Those, and a hundred other things. I love you for the understanding, the wisdom you show in so many ways. When I told you about my father—well, I've never forgotten the things you said to me that night. You said you thought I'd been warped at the age of eleven, when he committed suicide. You said that I might have grown up then, but I didn't *mature*, as I'd put it, that my taking such a biased view of women, of marriage, was not the sign of a mature, well-rounded person. You were right.'

He held on to her hands tightly. 'You were right, darling. That's why I didn't argue, why I had no answer for you. The thought wasn't new to me, Dawn. But before meeting you, I hadn't been able to change myself, to change my attitudes. That's because I'd never been in love, never loved a woman the way my father had loved, the way Richie loved. Only now, *now*, can I

understand what it feels like not to want to carry on
without someone you love so deeply. Obviously I've
always realised what a painful emotion love can be; it
destroyed my father and it almost destroyed my
brother. But I had never experienced it first hand, never
knew what it *feels* like. Now I do. Dear God, now I do!
I no longer feel towards my father that resentment I
told you about, the anger towards him. I no longer
think him a coward for not facing life. I understand, I
understand what a tremendous power love is.

'In other words, my darling girl, only now am I really
mature enough to discard what I have believed all these
years. It's taken all these years, Dawn, and you're
responsible for this change in me.'

He took her gently into his embrace and held her
very, very, close. 'I'm in your hands. My life, my heart,
is yours. I'm yielding gladly to the love I feel for you, so
please say you'll marry me, Dawn. Tell me again that
you love me, say you'll marry me and that we'll
continue to grow together for the rest of our lives.'

Through misty, loving eyes, Dawn looked at him and
said all of that. She said it word for word because more
than anything else in the world, she wanted that future
with Cosmo.

Harlequin *Presents*

Coming Next Month

895 STORM Vanessa Grant
After being stranded by a fierce storm in the Queen Charlotte Islands a reporter doubts herself, the hard-hitting pilot she desires and her commitment to a childhood sweetheart.

896 LOSER TAKE ALL Rosemary Hammond
A wealthy American doesn't exactly win his new bride in a poker game. But it amounts to the same thing, because it's marriage for them—win or lose!

897 THE HARD MAN Penny Jordan
Desire for a virtual stranger reminds a young widow and mother she is still a woman capable of love, capable of repeating the mistake she made ten years ago.

898 EXPLOSIVE MEETING Charlotte Lamb
A lab technician's boss resents his employee's impassioned plea on behalf of a brilliant scientist who keeps blowing up the lab. And he misinterprets her persistence—in more ways than one!

899 AN ALL-CONSUMING PASSION Anne Mather
When her father's right-hand man comes to the Caribbean to escort the boss's daughter back to London, she tries to make him forget his responsibilities—never thinking she is playing with fire.

900 LEAVING HOME Leigh Michaels
A young woman never dreams her guardian's decision to remain single had anything to do with her, until he proposes marriage—to pull her out of yet another scrape.

901 SUNSTROKE Elizabeth Oldfield
Can a widow reconcile receiving twenty thousand pounds to pay off her late husband's creditors with leaving the man she loves—even though he's been groomed to marry someone else?

902 DANGEROUS MOONLIGHT Kay Thorpe
It is possible that the Greek hotel owner a vacationer encounters isn't the same man who ruined her sister's marriage. But can she risk asking him outright, when the truth could break her heart?

Available in July wherever paperback books are sold, or through Harlequin Reader Service.

In the U.S.
901 Fuhrmann Blvd.
P.O. Box 1397
Buffalo, N.Y. 14240-1397

In Canada
P.O. Box 2800, Postal Station A
5170 Yonge Street
Willowdale, Ontario M2N 6J3

HARLEQUIN BRINGS YOU

Janet Dailey
★ ★ AMERICANA ★ ★ ★

A romantic tour of America with Janet Dailey!
★
Enjoy the first two releases of this collection of your favorite previously published Janet Dailey titles, presented alphabetically state by state.